Perfidy & Promises: A Pride & Prejudice Variation Mystery Romance

Crime & Courtship, Volume 5

Abbey North

Published by Abbey North JAFF Books, 2022.

PERFIDY & PROMISES: A PRIDE & PREJUDICE VARIATION MYSTERY ROMANCE

First edition. February 10, 2022.

ISBN: 979-8215966020

Written by Abbey North.

Blurb

Lizzy and her family arrive at Pemberley to allow Fitzwilliam a chance to court her. Things are off to a splendid start until Lady Catherine invites herself, and Caroline Bingley is clearly intent on causing trouble between ODC. Someone is targeting Fitzwilliam and Pemberley for harassment, but is it the same person who murders the stablemaster during Lizzy's stay? She and Darcy find themselves at odds over theories of the crime, but will that disagreement keep them from building a future together?

This is part five of the completed "Crime & Courtship" series. It is intended to be read in order and follow roughly the same timeline and location as J.A.'s masterpiece. The first mystery takes place in Meryton, then Netherfield, followed by Hunsford, then London, and finally Pemberley. The story arc continues throughout all five parts, compromising one long read broken into five sections. A mystery is central to each installment, so you could call this a cozy mystery sweet Regency romance.

While Abbey sometimes writes sensual JAFF, this series is strictly SWEET.

Chapter One

"**I** confess I still do not understand why we are visiting Mr. Darcy. The man is most unpleasant," said Fanny Bennet as the carriage hit another rut in the road that made them all jolt on the seat. "I am perplexed why he would issue this invitation, and further perplexed why you would accept, dear Lizzy."

"It is an opportunity for Jane to see Mr. Bingley." She had no intention of delving into her deeper and conflicting feelings for Mr. Darcy with her mother. If Fanny suspected she had any sort of affection for the man, she would likely be able to overcome her dislike of him in order to plot the best way to ensure a marriage between them. She didn't trust her mother with that goal.

"It is kind of you," said Lydia with a sniff. "I cannot bear to endure Mr. Darcy's company for that long."

"Yet you are here," said Kitty with a giggle.

Lizzy wished Jane were in the carriage with her, but her sister had ridden with Charles and Caroline Bingley. She wondered at Jane's ability to stand being confined to the carriage that long with Charles's sister, for it would have been a very unpleasant task indeed to Lizzy.

The Bingleys had traveled with them, since they were visiting Netherfield, and it was completely proper for Jane to be with them, since she had a chaperone. Considering the conversation Mr. Bingley had with Thomas Bennet shortly before they departed on their adventure for Pemberley, no one would object.

Lizzy's stomach clenched with nerves as they rounded the corner, and she got her first glimpse of Pemberley. The Lake District in general was splendidly beautiful, but Pemberley stood out as a distinction among all the natural wonders around her. It was the jewel of the crown, and she had a fluttering sensation in her chest as she imagined being mistress of it.

Of course, she had rejected Fitzwilliam's proposal so insultingly given at Hunsford, and there was no guarantee it would ever be issued again. She couldn't decide if she was relieved or disappointed by that. Everything about Mr. Darcy left her feeling conflicted and torn. He was full of pride and arrogance, but there was a softer side to him as well.

She certainly found no fault with his intelligence, deductive reasoning, or ability to carry on a conversation. He seemed to have withdrawn all objection to his friend Bingley marrying her sister, but she supposed they would soon know if that was true. She doubted he would be able to hide his genuine reaction when he learned the news.

Deciding to focus on that rather than how nervous she was at seeing him again, Lizzy smoothed her dress and touched the scar on her neck self-consciously. The surgeon had assured her it might eventually fade to be barely noticeable, but it was still visible at the moment, only a few weeks out from when Tristan Nobles had inflicted it upon her. She couldn't help being insecure about it, and her movement drew her mother's attention.

Fanny wailed anew at the sight of it. "Oh, that ugly mark. How you will ever find a husband who will overlook it bewilders me. I cannot believe you allowed yourself to be kidnapped and attacked."

Aunt Gardiner winced at her sister-in-law's words and sent Lizzy a sympathetic smile.

With what Lizzy hoped was an even tone, she said, "I would have certainly reconsidered had I realized how inconvenient it would be for you, Mama."

Kitty snickered as Fanny fanned herself, obviously not detecting Lizzy's sarcasm. "I do wish you would think things through. You are a bright girl, but far too impulsive."

Lizzy's mouth struggled to form a smile, requiring a great deal of control to suppress the urge. She found it both humorous and the height of hypocrisy to have her mother complaining about her impulsiveness when Lydia, Fanny's favorite daughter, was the very embodiment of the inclination itself. "Yes, Mama," she murmured softly.

Despite her nervousness, she was relieved when the carriage stopped moments later, hoping it would divert Fanny from the topic of her scar and her careless thoughtlessness at allowing it to come about. The door opened, and the groom assisted them down one at a time.

Lizzy was the second to last to leave the carriage, and when she stepped down, she saw Fitzwilliam waiting for her, along with Georgiana at his side. The Bingleys and Jane already stood waiting, their carriage having arrived moments before the Bennets', and while Fitzwilliam was greeting Bingley, his gaze remained on Lizzy. That fluttering sensation returned to her chest as she saw the warmth in his gaze, certain it was reflected in hers as well.

When it was finally her turn to greet Fitzwilliam, he took her hand and brought it to his mouth, holding a second longer than necessary. Even through the barrier of their gloves, she could feel the warmth of his skin, and it sent a frisson of pleasure down her spine.

"Welcome to Pemberley, Miss Lizzy." His eyes sparkled as he said the words. There was nothing improper about them, but she couldn't help recalling how it'd been in the Gardiners' sitting room weeks before, free to call him Fitzwilliam and him to call her Lizzy without any formalities between them.

"Thank you for having us, Mr. Darcy." She almost stumbled over the name, wishing she could use his given name instead.

After everyone had exchanged a greeting, the Darcys led them into the sitting room. "You must be parched after your journey," said Georgiana. "Servants will see to dispersal of your items, and Mrs.

Reynolds will show you to your rooms after you have had some refreshments."

Lizzy sat down, happy to have a seat that wasn't jolting underneath her. Three days in the carriage, especially with the company she'd kept, had been wearying, and she feared her bottom might remain permanently numb.

"Jane and I have news," said Bingley once chatter had died down for a moment. He was squaring his shoulders, and he seemed to be prepared for protest when he said, "Mr. Bennet has given us permission to marry."

Lizzy watched Fitzwilliam, holding her breath as she kept her teacup aloft without taking a sip. She was carefully watching every reaction, looking for something to betray his true opinion. He seemed relatively unbothered when he said, "Congratulations are in order then. I am sure you will bring each other much happiness."

Lizzy let out the breath she'd been holding and took a sip of her tea, relief filling her. His objections to Jane and Charles's union had been the main point of contention remaining between them. Now that he had given his blessing and was no longer meddling, it left Lizzy in the position of having to discover exactly how she felt about Fitzwilliam herself.

There could be no distraction based on his attitude toward her sister or others. It was thorny, to be sure. In some ways, she was certain how she felt, but hesitations remained. To her disappointment, she had no chance to speak with him alone during teatime. She was tempted to remain behind when the others went up with Mrs. Reynolds, but it wouldn't be proper.

Mrs. Reynolds led them upstairs, providing a tour of various items of interest. As they were in the elder Mr. Darcy's study, where Mrs. Reynolds assured them they could freely help themselves to the library within, since no one used the room any longer, Lizzy was startled to see a painting of George Wickham in his younger years arranged on the mantel of the fireplace alongside Fitzwilliam and Georgiana. She wasn't surprised the man had commissioned the painting of the younger George, since by all accounts he had been quite fond of him. She was slightly surprised that it remained, and she admired Fitzwilliam's restraint at not discarding it.

After Mrs. Reynolds had situated them all in their rooms, ignoring the grumbling protests of Kitty and Lydia for having to share while Lizzy and Jane both received their own rooms, Lizzy decided to take a nap. She hadn't rested well at the inns where they had stopped, and the bed was luxuriously soft.

SHE WOKE A COUPLE OF hours later and realized it was time to prepare for dinner. While she had been having tea, one of Pemberley's efficient servants had already unpacked her things, so she selected one of the three new dresses her mother had commissioned from Madam St. Croix for her. It had been an indulgence all the girls received, including Mary, though she wasn't coming along on the trip. Mary had certainly been invited, but newly betrothed, she had chosen to remain at Longbourn with Thomas so she could be near her fiancé.

After collecting her outfit for the evening, she slipped into Jane's room. They hadn't traveled with a lady's maid, and though Lizzy was certain there was one available at Pemberley if they requested it, the sisters were used to helping each other, so she assisted Jane with her hair before trading places with her so Jane could do the same.

They assisted each other with their stays, and then Lizzy picked up her dress. She had selected her favorite among the new ones, a simple white dress with embroidered rosettes across the bustline, which was a tad lower than she normally accepted. She considered using a fichu but decided against it. After donning a matching sleeveless robe in the same vibrant pink as the rosettes embroidered across the bodice, Lizzy slipped on her gloves and waited for Jane. When her sister was dressed in a light-blue evening dress that highlighted her eyes, they exited her room.

They walked down the stairs arm in arm, both quickly getting turned around despite Mrs. Reynolds's excellent tour earlier. Fortunately, they came across Mr. Bingley and his sister, and though Caroline was clearly dismayed, Charles lit up at the sight of them. To be fair, mainly at the sight of Jane, but Lizzy could hardly fault him for that.

She relinquished her sister's arm so Mr. Bingley could take it, and he led them through the house. It was obvious he was familiar with Pemberley, but Lizzy was gratified to see Caroline hesitated at different points, waiting for her brother to lead them.

That suggested she had been an infrequent guest at Pemberley, which pleased Lizzy. It was no secret Caroline wanted to be Mrs. Fitzwilliam Darcy, and though Lizzy had heard for herself directly from Fitzwilliam that he had no interest in assisting Caroline with the aspirations, it was still a relief to know he hadn't invited the other woman to his home very often.

Lizzy was disappointed not to get to sit near Fitzwilliam at dinner either. They barely exchanged a few words, and she was frustrated by their lack of interaction. She attempted to pay attention to the conversations happening around her, and at least she was seated beside Georgiana.

Georgiana was still on the shy side, but she seemed to have gained some new confidence, perhaps because of their previous acquaintance. She seemed to favor Lizzy over the others nearby, including Kitty and Lydia, but she suspected that was simply because she was more comfortable with Lizzy.

After dinner, the women excused themselves to go into the salon, and Mrs. Reynolds quickly brought in trays of tea. Lizzy was impatient for the men to join them, but she tried to hide it as she sat beside Georgiana on the settee and accepted a cup of tea.

"He is very happy, you know?"

Lizzy looked up at the statement. "Pardon?"

Georgiana smiled. "My brother. He has been happier of late than I recall in a long time, if ever. I do believe he is in love," she said in a meaningful fashion.

Lizzy almost smiled in response, but seeing Caroline Bingley in the armchair beside Georgiana, avidly listening without any attempt at subtlety, curtailed the reaction. "How lovely for him," she said instead in a neutral voice.

Georgiana frowned. "I do believe he is on the verge of making an offer."

Lizzy could have enlightened her that he'd already done so, but she was as eager as Fitzwilliam likely was to forget about the insulting proposal he had issued. The opinions he'd harbored then still stung, but she was hopeful his viewpoint had changed in the intervening months.

"How have you been, Elizabeth?" asked Georgiana.

"I have been well. How have you been?" She wanted to ask about Georgiana's continued recovery from the abduction, but there seemed little need. The young woman appeared to have rebounded from the experience, and there was a new liveliness about her that suggested she bore no long-term trauma from the event.

"I am fine." She smiled for a moment before her expression darkened. "Our party is not complete yet."

Lizzy arched a brow, wondering who else might be arriving. Even as Georgiana said the words, she realized who was possibly missing, and she found herself fervently hoping Georgiana would say Richard Fitzwilliam's name.

Instead, she said, "Lady Catherine and Miss Anne are coming to visit, and they should arrive tomorrow." There was sympathy in her gaze.

Lizzy did her best to hide a grimace in her teacup, not missing the way Caroline sneered in delight. There could only be one reason

Lady Catherine would intrude, and she must have gotten word from someone there was a possible romance developing between Lizzy and Fitzwilliam.

Since the woman was determined to see Fitzwilliam married to Anne despite both her daughter and her nephew's lack of interest in the idea, she would immediately act to forestall any progression of affection between Darcy and any other woman, but particularly someone like Lizzy Bennet.

Lizzy took a deep sip of her tea, almost wishing it were something more bracing, as she girded herself to battle with Lady Catherine. Of course, it couldn't be a simple trip to Pemberley that would allow her to just focus on her feelings for Fitzwilliam. At least no one had died, been kidnapped, or blackmailed since her arrival. The odds of such a crime occurring again were astronomical, were they not?

Chapter Two

Lizzy had some time alone with Fitzwilliam the next morning, having risen early for breakfast. It was her natural inclination anyway, but she recalled from their stay at Netherfield that he kept similar hours, and her hope had paid off when she entered the dining room and found him receiving a plate.

She sat down and placed her order with the maid, who turned to her after delivering Mr. Darcy's plate, and she waited until they were alone. She was unable to quell the impulse to reach out and put her hand over his. "Finally, a few moments alone."

He looked regretful. "That is the difficulty with having a large house party. I would much rather have you to myself."

Lizzy flushed at the words, and pleasure suffused her. She smiled at him, and his grin, so open and vulnerable, clearly revealing the depths of his feelings for her, nudged her ever closer to embracing the affection she felt for him. "I suppose it would be improper with just the two of us." She let out a long sigh.

"Under the current circumstances, of course."

Lizzy didn't look at him as she poured herself a cup of tea, wondering if he were alluding to the idea that if they were married, no one would care if they were there alone. It was an appealing thought, but she was still uncertain.

"Are you truly accepting of Mr. Bingley and Jane's engagement?" she asked after the maid had brought her plate and departed.

He looked up from his dish with surprise, brows furrowing. "I am. Did I come across as insincere?" He seemed troubled by that.

She quickly shook her head. "No, but I wanted to be sure. I prefer honesty between us. If you still have any reservations—"

He scowled lightly. "I do not, as I said in London. I suspect you want to hear me say it again, so I will indulge you. I was wrong."

Lizzy smiled, admitting part of her enjoyed hearing him say that, but she was mostly just happy from relief. "I am glad you reevaluated your opinion and withdrew your objections, Fitzwilliam."

"How could I not when she clearly makes Charles happy, and he seems to make Miss Jane equally happy?" He sipped his tea before saying, "Speaking of happiness, or a lack thereof, I fear I must brace you for something."

"No doubt, you refer to Lady Catherine's impending arrival?" Lizzy was proud of how unconcerned she sounded.

His eyes widened, and he nodded. "I take it Georgiana revealed the news?"

"She did." Lizzy sipped the tea before taking a bite of the excellently poached eggs. "I confess to a lack of enthusiasm, but I shall endure."

He looked troubled despite her confident tone. "I feel I must warn you she is likely here to interfere. No doubt, my aunt has heard certain rumors about...us, and she is likely here to try to prevent any advancement."

Lizzy smiled at him, still feeling a touch concerned, but she was mostly as confident as she sounded when she said, "I do not intimidate easily, Fitzwilliam, and while your aunt is a fearsome lady, I am not overly concerned."

She had expected him to be relieved, but he continued to frown. "Do not underestimate her, Lizzy. She is ruthless, particularly when it comes to getting what she desires. She is unlikely to accept I will not marry Anne until either the day Anne or I marry someone else. Even then, it would not surprise me if she tried to scheme against my spouse or Anne's."

Lizzy shook her head. "Surely, even Lady Catherine would have to admit she had been bested at that point?"

He still seemed uncertain. "I would like to believe that, but the lady does like to get her way."

Lizzy didn't dismiss his warning, but she wasn't as concerned about it as he was. Once she had decided her own mind, she knew she would stick with that. She was already leaning toward falling in love with Fitzwilliam, and if the proper environment existed to lead her all the way down that path, Lady Catherine would be an obstacle in her way, but she wouldn't be enough to deter Lizzy when she decided what she wanted to do.

LIZZY WAS PART OF THE welcoming group waiting when Lady Catherine's carriage pulled up the long drive of Pemberley. The Fitzwilliam family crest was on the door, though Lizzy would have expected it to be Lewis de Bourgh's instead. Perhaps Lady Catherine had changed it after her husband's death to remind everyone she was the daughter of an Earl.

Lizzy was startled to see a familiar face when the driver got down, and she realized Carlos was the one driving the carriage. She nodded to him subtly when their gazes locked, and he gave her an equally subtle nod before hurrying to the carriage to open the door for Lady Catherine, who exited first. Anne came next, and Lizzy didn't miss the extra careful way Carlos handed her down, hand on her elbow for a moment longer than necessary before she stepped away from him, and he closed the carriage door to return to his perch and drive it to the carriage house.

"What an assembly," said Lady Catherine. The tone wasn't flattering, particularly when her gaze settled on Lizzy for a moment longer than required. There was clear dislike in her expression, and

Lizzy trembled slightly under the force of it, understanding perhaps a little better now why Fitzwilliam was so apprehensive on her behalf.

Lizzy was able to escape shortly enough after a brief greeting with all of them, and she invited Anne to walk with her when the other woman complained her back was twinging from the long carriage ride. They skipped tea in favor of the walk, crossing the beautiful grounds of Pemberley arm in arm as they discussed inconsequential matters until they were out of the hearing range of everyone assembled in front of the house.

"How are you?" asked Lizzy as soon as it was safe to do so. "Has Mr. Collins made any further overtures to demand money?"

Anne grinned. "Indeed, he has not. In fact, the few times I have been forced to interact with him, he is eager to keep his gaze on the ground, and his face flushes. He starts to sweat, and thrice now, his poor wife has thought he must be suffering from some ailment."

Lizzy laughed along with Anne, not begrudging the other woman some pleasure in her cousin's reaction. The man had blackmailed her, after all, so who could blame her? "I am relieved to hear that. Fitzwilliam issued some threats I have no doubt will haunt Mr. Collins every time he thinks of them for the rest of his life."

Anne surprised her by flopping down onto the grass. "You must tell me all about it. We did not have a chance to fully discuss the matter after you and Fitzwilliam settled it at Rosings Park."

Happily, Lizzy joined her on the grass, relaying the scene of the confrontation with Mr. Collins. She had practically memorized Fitzwilliam's words, since she'd been so impressed by his ability to cow the other man, and she related them with relish now.

Anne hung on every word, clearly enraptured, and they both agreed Fitzwilliam was a formidable man when crossed. "It is a good thing he likes you," said Anne in a teasing tone.

Lizzy stiffened, uncomfortable at the acknowledgment. Of course, she hadn't shared Mr. Darcy had offered that bumbling proposal shortly after their confrontation with Mr. Collins, and she doubted Anne had any special knowledge of the event. No doubt, Fitzwilliam was eager to keep the incident to himself, and Lizzy hadn't told anyone besides Jane. "We have developed a good working relationship together," she said primly. "He has a great mind for solving intrigues, and I have appreciated his assistance."

Anne clearly wasn't buying it. She snickered. "Of course, that is all there is to it," she said with gentle mocking.

Lizzy took it in stride, nodding. "Of course."

Anne leaned back then, staring up at the sky. "I am growing frustrated. I suspect my mother is aware I have been sneaking out, though I do not think she knows why. She insisted on rearranging my wing of the house, and Mrs. Jenkinson's quarters are much closer to mine now. You cannot believe how relieved I was when she chose to take a trip to see her sister instead of coming along with us. I do adore the old dear, but she is complicating the situation and denying me happiness. All at my mother's behest."

Anne sounded so miserable that Lizzy couldn't help reaching out to squeeze her hand in a comforting fashion as she laid down beside her. "We must do something to remedy that. I am certain there must be a building currently not in use on Pemberley lands. I suggest we find it, and then I shall deliver a note to Carlos for you to ensure there is no witness to you visiting him during the day. You can arrange a meeting time with him, and I will escort you there and then walk back with you afterward. In the meantime, I shall occupy myself by doing other things."

Anne beamed, clearly excited at the possibility. "You would do that?"

"Of course, I would. I suggest we resume our walk and find a suitable location for your assignation."

Anne bounded to her feet, apparently able to overcome the twinging in her back with the advent of their goal, and Lizzy stood up to join her. It took almost an hour to find a suitable building, but they discovered a cottage that appeared uninhabited.

Mr. Darcy must be between tenants at the moment, but it could not have been long, for there was only a slightly disused air about it, and though the bedsheets were musty, and there was a little dust on everything, it was not so neglected that it would prove to be too great a barrier to overcome for Anne's purposes.

They returned to the house, whispering together before parting in the foyer as Anne promised to write the note immediately and get it to Lizzy within an hour, so she could arrange a visit to the stables to deliver it. As promised, it was in Lizzy's hands less than thirty minutes later, and she went for yet another walk, this one taking her deliberately to the stables.

Carlos was there, but he was in the company of an older man Lizzy soon learned was Alfred Terrence, the stablemaster. He had a calm and competent air about him, and Lizzy could understand why the horses seemed to like him so well.

He offered to saddle one of Darcy's horses for her, but Lizzy demurred, sharing regretfully that she wasn't much of a horsewoman. When he was preoccupied for a moment, she slipped the note to Carlos and carried on with her walk, soon returning to the house. She felt no need to wait for a reply, for she was certain Carlos would find a way to excuse himself to meet Anne at the rendezvous point the next morning.

THE NEXT DAY, ASSURED Anne was in good hands with Carlos, Lizzy left them at the cottage and began to wander the grounds of Pemberley. The walk she'd taken with Anne yesterday had allowed her to learn some of its wonders, but they had been more focused on the task of finding a suitable meeting spot for an assignation than appreciating the natural marvels around them. Lizzy lost herself in the magnificence of the landscape as she walked along, issuing a sigh of regret that Longbourn wasn't quite this lovely.

She was preoccupied with her thoughts, so she didn't see Lady Catherine until she had already rounded the curve of the path and noticed the older woman waiting there. Her heart skipped a beat as she wondered if Lady Catherine was looking for her daughter.

The idea of the daunting woman finding Anne *in flagrante delicto* with her groom almost made Elizabeth's blood run cold. Forcing a cheerful smile, she approached Lady Catherine, hoping to divert her from that direction. "Good morning, Lady Catherine. It is an excellent time for a walk."

The older woman sniffed. "It is only through being apprised that you often wake at such an ungodly hour to meander the grounds like a common waif has roused me from my bed and set me on this course."

Lizzy wasn't certain if she should be relieved that Catherine wasn't looking for Anne, or if she should be alarmed that she was apparently the older woman's quarry. She decided she could feel both, though she strove to keep her expression pleasant. "How flattering. I cannot imagine for what reason you would seek me out, but shall we walk?"

After a moment, Lady Catherine fell into step beside her, and Lizzy pointedly turned from the direction of the cottage, keeping up her original trajectory to bring Catherine as far away from it as possible. "Was there something you wished to discuss, Lady Catherine?"

"Your family is the most disagreeable sort."

Lizzy's shoulders stiffened slightly, but she made no comment.

"Your mother has frightful manners, and the man I sent to look into your family tells me you are all eccentric. Your father can barely be bothered to leave his library, and he clearly failed to ensure your mother raised you properly."

"My father is a kind and wonderful man, and he values books more than he does the silly notions of the *ton*." Lizzy could handle much but criticizing Thomas Bennet wouldn't stand.

"Such impertinence. Yet my man also turned up the information that you and Jane Bennet are tolerably well behaved and appear to be the best of the lot from the Bennet family. Mr. Collins holds Miss Jane in high opinion, though he is more ambivalent about you."

"That is hardly surprising, since I rejected his proposal three years ago." Lizzy made no attempt to hide the annoyance in her tone.

The lady stumbled for a moment, clearly shocked by the idea. "Mr. Collins deigned to ask for your hand, and you refused him? What foolishness."

"I did not love him, and it is obvious Charlotte makes a far better wife for Mr. Collins than I ever could."

There was actually a hint of affection on Lady Catherine's face for moment as she nodded. "I cannot disagree with that. Mrs. Collins is a biddable woman, and she enhances Mr. Collins's happiness."

"Then we are agreed. I made the best decision." Lizzy strove to sound cheerful, though she feared she sounded mindless more than anything.

Lady Catherine was apparently not finished with the topic. "I have heard of some of your scandalous behavior."

Lizzy frowned. "What scandalous behavior would that be, Lady Catherine?" For the most part, Lizzy was a paragon of propriety. Or, she gave every appearance of being anyway.

"Mucking about in the countryside in pursuit of a thief. Constable Walters was happy to tell my man all about your shameful behavior, and the way you insisted on inserting yourself into his investigation."

Lizzy laughed. "Constable Walters is hardly a good judge of character, and he could not find his hat with his hand." She remembered the phrase Mr. Cravvy had used and borrowed liberally. "I had the audacity to suggest he should actually do his job, and therefore, the man considers me a hoyden."

Lady Catherine sniffed. "Truthfully, I do not care about the petty dramas that plague Longbourn and Meryton. What matters to me is the most disturbing rumor I have heard."

Lizzy was certain she knew what was coming, since Lady Catherine had gone to all the effort to send someone to investigate Lizzy and her family, and she had inserted herself into the Pemberley party during Lizzy's visit. Still, she refused to make it easy for Lady Catherine. "Rumors do fly all the time, so perhaps you could elucidate?"

"I am referring to the perfectly ridiculous idea that my nephew, Anne's betrothed, is planning to offer for your hand."

Lizzy spared her a small smile. "It does sound utterly ridiculous, does it not?"

Lady Catherine didn't appear assuaged by her words. "I could hardly credit the idea."

"Yet here you are, prepared to intercede to keep it from happening. I suppose you must have given it at least a small amount of credit."

The lady sneered. "Of course not. I am simply here to ensure you do not try to act on such rumors and encourage a *tendre* that does not exist."

"I am well aware of what might or might not exist, Lady Catherine, and I assure you, I do not require you to tell me how I should behave, or what I should believe."

"You are such a sharp-tongued harridan. It is a wonder anyone could come up with the fiction of you being involved with Fitzwilliam to start with."

"I did find him rather helpful in solving the theft at Meryton, along with other matters we have investigated." Lizzy had no intention of revealing Anne's extortion, or Georgiana's abduction, but if Catherine pressed her, she would be happy to tell her all about the murderer they had stopped in London, but unfortunately not before he claimed more victims.

The woman looked like she might be close to apoplexy. "Such audacious lies. You should be ashamed of yourself. Even someone as low-born and common as you, with no proper upbringing, must know how improper it is to spread untruths."

"I find this conversation tiresome, Lady Catherine. If you have a point, I would like you to get to it. Otherwise, I shall wish you a good day and part."

"Has Fitzwilliam asked for your hand in marriage?"

Lizzy had no intention of discussing her private business with the woman, especially revealing the proposal that had occurred at Hunsford. She found herself oddly protective of Fitzwilliam too, aware how his aunt would take the news, and how it might alter her opinion of Fitzwilliam. "You yourself have already declared the idea preposterous, so how could you bear it any weight?"

That seemed to satisfy the woman, and she nodded. "That is as I suspected. Gossips do like to hear the sound of their own voices, and they do not care if they are relaying the truth."

Lizzy felt it prudent not to answer.

Lady Catherine apparently didn't realize or care that Lizzy hadn't made a response. "I wish to secure your promise that if my nephew were ever to do something so ridiculous, you would immediately reject his offer."

"It is as ludicrous to make promises about future events that might never occur as it is to speculate about them to start with."

The woman frowned. "Do you promise?"

"Allow me to reassure you, Lady Catherine, that I know my own mind and will make my own decision if such an impossible situation occurred."

Her lips pursed with disapproval. "I should hardly be surprised, for you must be a grasping social climber just like your sister, who has latched herself onto the tradesman, Bingley. Still, I had hoped you had some modicum of decency, and you would not attempt to try to lure away an engaged man."

"Certainly, if Mr. Darcy is engaged to Miss Anne, it would be highly unlikely he would ever propose to start with? Do you not agree?"

The woman's eyes darted around, and she looked uncomfortable for a moment. "It is not yet a formally announced betrothal. It is more of an understanding."

Lizzy arched her brow. "Oh, how do you mean?" she asked politely, phrasing it as though she only had academic curiosity.

Lady Catherine shifted slightly, perhaps unconsciously revealing her discomfort with the topic. "His mother and I used to plan for our children to be joined from the time they were both in leading strings. It is only a matter of formality now."

"I suppose Fitzwilliam and Anne would agree?"

Lady Catherine seemed annoyed, and Lizzy couldn't decide if it was because she dared challenge the woman even subtly, or because she'd use the first name of both Anne and Fitzwilliam without apology.

"It is understood by all parties involved. Now, I ask you again, will you maintain honor as a proper woman should and decline any sort of involvement with my nephew should he offer? I suppose you would make a tolerable mistress, but you could never be his wife."

Lizzy blinked, uncertain how to respond. "You have no objection if I were Mr. Darcy's mistress while he was married to your daughter?"

Catherine sneered. "I am certain my nephew could do better even for a bit of muslin, but that is the way of marriage. My daughter will be practical enough to understand that. Do you promise me you will decline any offer of marriage from Fitzwilliam?"

Lizzy straightened her shoulders. "I shall not make a promise to you about anything, Lady Catherine. All I promise to do is follow my heart. Now if you shall excuse me, I intend to enjoy my walk in solitude." Without waiting for a reply, she turned and veered to the right, departing from the path in the hopes Lady Catherine wouldn't risk damaging her slippers by following.

Her gamble paid off, for the woman didn't bother to follow her, and Lizzy took a wide circle around the property, making her way back to the cottage more than an hour later. She wasn't certain if she should knock on the door, but she did clear her throat outside loudly, and the door opened moments later with Anne appearing.

She looked as impeccably dressed as she had before, but her cheeks were flushed with color, and there was a pleased sparkle in her eye that Lizzy couldn't help envying. It was obvious spending time with her lover had reinvigorated her, and Lizzy found herself thinking more of Fitzwilliam than usual as she and Anne returned to the house.

Chapter Three

The smell of smoke woke Lizzy, and a quick glance out her window revealed a fire across the grounds. It seemed to be coming from the stables, and she quickly threw on her night-rail and shoved her feet into slippers as she hurried into the hallway. Other guests had gathered as well, save for Lady Catherine, and they all rushed downstairs.

Even her mother was in attendance, and Fanny made no complaint as Mr. Darcy directed them all to line up to join the bucket brigade. First, he selected Mr. Bingley and a few of the male servants to help him enter the stables and bring out the horses.

Lizzy stood by Anne, who seemed poised to run in. Lizzy was certain she was concerned for her horses, but she was obviously far more concerned for Carlos. Keeping her voice low, she said, "Only the stablemaster sleeps in the stables, and only at his discretion. Carlos will have his own quarters."

Anne nodded, seeming to cling to the hope, and there was a tortured sob that escaped her when Carlos emerged moments later leading two horses by the reins.

As soon as the men had emptied the stables of the horses, they joined the line as well. There was nothing so egalitarian as trying to put out a fire, and the group worked as seamlessly as possible for the next two hours to extinguish the flames before they could spread to the nearby foliage, other outbuildings, or reach Pemberley's main house.

While in the midst of it, Lizzy hadn't realized how exhausted she was, but once they were done passing buckets, her arms trembled, and her chest ached. There was a spasm in her back, and she longed for nothing more than a soak in a hot tub, though that was a luxury she wouldn't request tonight. After all the work the servants had done alongside them, she could hardly expect them to carry in the copper tub and multiple pails of hot water.

She would have to content herself with washing up in the basin, and she thought longingly of the spring that flowed near their house at Longbourn. Her mother had long ago deemed she and her sisters too old to swim there, but that didn't stop them most of the time on a hot summer's day. Even though it would be a cool experience plunging into the water at night, she wished she had the opportunity now.

Furtive whispers caught her attention, and she realized one of the servants was quietly consulting with Mr. Darcy. Lizzy moved closer without even trying to hide she was eavesdropping. Fitzwilliam shot her a look, but he didn't dissuade her, and she learned soon enough there was a body in the stables. "Your stablemaster didn't escape the fire?" She felt a wave of sadness for the man she had met earlier.

Darcy nodded to his servant, excusing him before putting a hand on Lizzy's arm. "It appears the stablemaster was dead before the fire began." He lowered his voice. "He has been stabbed through the heart."

Lizzy's eyes widened. "I take it there is not much to be gleaned from the remnants?" How could one pose that question delicately?

He hesitated and then shook his head. "I very much doubt you would see anything that would lead you to finding a clue."

She let out a sigh of relief at not having to ask to examine the body. "Have you sent for the constable?"

Fitzwilliam nodded. "I have, and Constable Smith is passably competent. I have also sent one of my people to fetch a Runner. I am hopeful Mr. Kenton will visit Pemberley at my behest."

Lizzy frowned. "If your constable is competent, do you really believe we need a Runner?"

"It is not just the question of how Mr. Terrence came to have a knife through his heart. There have been other incidences of late that make me suspect someone is targeting Pemberley."

She frowned. "Such as?"

"Last week, one of the grooms discovered my saddle had been cut. Not completely, but enough to fray loose and likely send me to my death if I were in the middle of a rapid ride, as I enjoy most days of the week."

Lizzy scowled at that news. "Someone tried to kill you?"

He hesitated, but then he nodded. "The evidence suggests that, for certain."

"What other incidents?"

"Several different servants have come to me to report seeing a shadowy figure skulking about the grounds at various times of the day and night. I have had no luck yet catching the person, but I trust the accounts and the people giving them."

Lizzy nodded. "Of course you do, especially with more than one giving the same story. Have there been other incidences?"

"There was a dead rat left on my bed several days ago." Fitzwilliam shuddered slightly. "It had not simply died of natural causes. I shall spare you the details, but suffice to say, someone had left it in a gruesome display. It was a threat, I am certain."

"I see the wisdom in sending for a Runner. Do you know who might wish you harm?"

Fitzwilliam's mouth tightened. "I can think of only one person, and you know him as well."

Lizzy bit her lip for a moment before she said, "George Wickham." It certainly made sense that he would be on a campaign for revenge, but was he really so shortsighted as to come back to Pemberley to torture Darcy when he could have had a chance to escape the country? "Would he be so imprudent to do such a thing? I understand there is acrimony between you, but would he not have left Britain entirely if he had the chance?"

"That is what an intelligent man would do. Wickham is certainly intelligent, but he lacks logic. He is prone to be ruled by his emotions rather than rationality, and it would not surprise me at all to learn he had squandered his chance to escape in favor of returning to Pemberley to make my life hell."

She frowned. "But why would he target poor Mr. Terrence?" She remembered the kindly man she'd met yesterday, and another pang went through her. "Did he have some personal issue with your stablemaster?"

"I do not see how. Mr. Terrence came to Pemberley about a year after Wickham's banishment. To my knowledge, the two never even met, but that is not to say there is not something existing between them. Or perhaps, Mr. Terrence was simply collateral damage, a burden Wickham had to deal with before he could freely set the fire."

Lizzy frowned. "That does not seem like Wickham."

His eyebrows drew together in a heavy scowl. "You do not believe Wickham would commit murder? What of my saddle?"

Lizzy hesitated. "Perhaps he would kill you. What I meant to say though, is it seems rather bold and far too direct an action for the Wickham I know. He is more inclined to prowl about, torturing you from the shadows. Perhaps he had an opportunity to cut your saddle and did so, but that is a rather hands-off way to kill someone. Waiting for the leather to inevitably break and not have to witness the results of his actions firsthand seems quite different than confronting someone and stabbing them directly."

He appeared to think about it for a moment before shaking his head. "I must disagree. He is certainly sly, but if pushed into a corner, I have no doubt he would act to save himself or to follow the course he had set."

"Nevertheless, I felt we should look into other matters concerning Mr. Terrence, just to ensure we are not overlooking a suspect." She sounded so confident that she was proud of herself. After the incident in London, when Mr. Nobles had managed to kidnap her and almost kill her, she was afraid her confidence in investigating might have been forever marred, so it was good to feel a spark of interest at the challenge ahead of her, though she loathed that the opportunity existed at the cost of a man's life.

Fitzwilliam frowned. "I believe we would be better served waiting for the Runner."

She frowned at him. "It will take two or three days for Mr. Kenton to arrive, and we might lose all information or hope of finding it by then. Perhaps, we might even have the murder solved by the time Mr. Kenton arrives, and then he can focus on catching Wickham."

Lizzy still thought the two crimes might not necessarily both lay at Wickham's feet, though she doubted Fitzwilliam was capable of seeing that possibility. She couldn't fault him for having a blind spot when it came to Wickham, for the man had done dastardly deeds, but she still thought he was far too cowardly to murder someone so directly.

When he didn't speak for a moment, she said, "Well, are you going to help me?"

Chapter Four

Fitzwilliam hesitated about answering for a moment, but he'd already cast the dye the moment he took her into his confidence. There was no denying Lizzy had a talent for this sort of thing, and together, they were a strong team.

With a small sigh, he nodded. "Of course, I shall assist you." His lips twitched at the idea he was assisting her. He preferred to view it as a partnership, but he suspected Lizzy regarded him as more of a subordinate. It was an unusual situation for a man like him, but he wasn't going to quibble with her about status.

"I suggest we begin by speaking with the people who work daily with Mr. Terrence." Lizzy had seemed exhausted after they put out the fire, and Fitzwilliam felt the same, but now she appeared reinvigorated as she started walking toward what was left of the stables. He put out a hand to stop her, saying in a low voice, "If you wish to speak to the grooms, they are with the horses."

Lizzy flushed, and then she laughed slightly. "Of course, they are. Why would they be in the burned-out stables?" She looked sad for a moment. "Not only has this incident cost you a fine man, but a fine building as well. What shall you do with the horses?"

"I am certain my men can rig up some sort of temporary shelter for them, and I will have to engage a builder to put up new stables as quickly as possible, at least before fall when the weather starts to turn. The horses will no doubt be all right in the interim."

She nodded, clearly satisfied with his plan, and headed in the direction of the horses in the field. Fitzwilliam followed her as the other guests started to dissipate, heading back to the house. Only Jane seemed slightly surprised that Lizzy was approaching the horses and the grooms with Mr. Darcy in tow. Apparently, her mother and other sisters were too exhausted to realize there was anything strange about Lizzy's behavior.

Lizzy approached the one Darcy pointed out as having worked there the longest, even preceding Mr. Terrence's arrival. She went to him first, and having learned his name from Fitzwilliam, she said, "I am sorry for your loss, Mr. Wirth."

The older man seemed surprised by her compassionate tone. He moved forward with a pronounced limp, which was the main reason he had declined the offer of becoming stablemaster when the position had opened nine years ago, according to Fitzwilliam. "It is my loss and everyone's," said the man in a gruff tone. "Mr. Terrence was a fine gentleman, and he had a way with the horses."

"You must have been good friends, having worked together for so long," said Lizzy.

Mr. Wirth nodded. "Indeed, we were."

"Can you think of anyone who might want to harm Mr. Terrence?"

Darcy observed it for himself that several of the grooms froze for a moment, and Mr. Wirth's gaze shifted slightly to the side. "I don't know what you are talking about, miss."

"Perhaps you are not aware yet, but Mr. Terrence was killed before the fire was set."

That caused the men around them to stiffen, and Mr. Wirth's bushy eyebrows drew together like two caterpillars intent on rendezvousing. "Are you saying someone murdered Mr. Terrence and then burned down the stables to cover it up?"

"That is one theory we are working on," said Darcy as he stepped forward. "We are not certain, other than we know Mr. Terrence was not killed in the fire." There was hardly any point in trying to keep it quiet, for word would leak soon enough, and he felt it was better for the servants to hear it from him. "Someone stabbed Mr. Terrence, so it was unlikely he was alive when the fire started."

"That does make sense," said one of the younger grooms.

"How so?" asked Lizzy.

"With all the sabotage that has been happening lately, and someone trying to light fire to the servants' cottage with the thatched roof last week, Mr. Terrence was concerned for the horses. He was afraid someone might try to tamper with the stables, so he had taken to sleeping in the quarters off the tack room instead of his usual apartment. If he'd been alive when the fire started, he would have done his best to put it out. I doubt it would have ever reached such a rowing blaze."

"I concur," said Mr. Wirth. "It is entirely conceivable Mr. Terrence would have lingered too long in the fire trying to put it out to save the horses, but if he had been alive when it started, he never would have allowed it to become the conflagration it did."

"That means someone killed Mr. Terrence, either because they wanted to set fire to the stables, or because they had a personal grievance with him." Lizzy tipped her head slightly.

Fitzwilliam suddenly found it amusing that she was standing in her night-rail and slippers interrogating his grooms, and seemingly without a hint of self-consciousness about it. Of course, she was amply covered, and her modesty was intact, but he admired that she could set aside such concerns to focus on far more important tasks. It was one of the many things he liked about her.

"Do you think the figure that has been creeping around Pemberley had it in for Mr. Terrence?" asked one of the grooms.

Darcy shook his head. "I believe that is a separate matter, though I have not ruled out the possibility both acts were done by the same person. I suspect Mr. Terrence might have simply been in the way and dealt with so the person could enact his plan to burn down the stables."

"I do disagree slightly with Mr. Darcy, at least in theory." Lizzy spoke with calm confidence, apparently uncaring or unaware of the undercurrent of unease her words caused.

Fitzwilliam could well imagine the surprise and perhaps even outrage among the men that she would dare disagree with him, their employer, and a man of his standing. She was clearly unintimidated by that, and she stared them down in turn. "In case there is a possibility the two actions are not related, I feel we must look into Mr. Terrence's personal life. Otherwise, we would never condone such an intrusion, but I hope you gentlemen can help us. Is there someone who would wish him harm?"

Mr. Wirth took a step forward. "I do not say that there is someone who would wish him harm, but he did spend a lot of time at the tavern in Lambton. If you go to the *Boar's Tusk*, they might be able to give you more information, miss." He nodded his head respectfully as he said that.

"Thank you for the information, Mr. Wirth." Lizzy straightened her shoulders. "I do believe those are all the questions I have for now, but I would ask you to make yourselves available if the need arises for further inquiries."

Since Lizzy wasn't looking at him, Darcy nodded subtly to indicate his support, though he wouldn't have been surprised if she'd been able to acquire their cooperation on her own even without any official authority over them. She could be persuasive, and her confidence was difficult to ignore.

"The horses should be all right for tonight, so everyone, get some rest. Tomorrow, I would like you to focus on trying to build them a makeshift shelter while I send to London for a builder." Darcy issued the orders to the men and nodded before taking Lizzy's arm to escort her back to the house. He wondered if she felt as bone-weary as he did, and he was certain she did, because her steps were slower and slower as they reached the steps of Pemberley.

"What I would not give for a bath," said Lizzy with a hint of wistfulness.

"That would be most refreshing."

"Of course, I would never burden the servants with that request tonight after everyone has worked so hard. I was thinking of the spring at Longbourn and wondering if you have such an option here, Mr. Darcy?"

His eyes widened at the suggestion. He cleared his throat as he shifted in his Hessians, aware his pants were growing tight at just the idea of her bathing in the moonlight. He cleared his throat. "There is a pond. I can show you where and keep watch for you."

She smiled at him, looking thankful as she nodded eagerly. "I would be most appreciative. You will not tell anyone, will you, Mr. Darcy?" she asked with an impish smile. "We both know how improper the request is."

"I shall not say a word, on my honor." It wasn't simply to preserve her reputation. The idea of sharing with anyone else that Lizzy had bathed in the pond with him standing nearby was knowledge he didn't want to reveal. He didn't want to risk anyone else envisioning the image in their minds, an image of which he felt far too possessive.

They were both still tired, but they managed the walk to the pond, which was a good half-mile from Pemberley. As promised, he turned away from her, holding her night-rail and refusing even to take a small peek. The temptation was strong, and he was happy to have conquered the impulse as he heard her splash around in the water.

Several minutes later, she emerged, reaching out a hand in front of him. He could see her bare arm, still wet with rivulets from the pond, and he quickly handed over her night-rail, maintaining his averted gaze.

When she appeared before him a moment later, she was wrapped in the night-rail and carrying her sodden night dress. He assumed she must have worn it into the water and then removed it upon finishing her wash. Her hair hung around her face in damp brown waves, and he longed to reach out and touch them. That would be a violation of trust, and beyond all bounds of propriety, despite how far they had already stepped outside them this evening.

She smiled. "Would you like me to stand guard for you while you take a swim, Fitzwilliam?"

He was alarmed at the prospect of disrobing around Lizzy. It wasn't that he feared she would sneak a peek, but because he wasn't certain he could manage his own impulses when the last vestiges hiding his reaction disappeared. It would be far harder to control himself if he were naked, and she wore only the one layer. He shook his head and cleared his throat. "I believe I am too tired for the endeavor. I shall simply settle for a washbasin of cold water."

She accepted his words without protest, taking his arm when he offered it. Her sleeve was slightly damp, but it wasn't enough to be bothersome.

They returned to the house without speaking, and he escorted her to the stairs that would lead to her wing. He thought about accompanying her to her door, which would have been the polite thing to do, but he feared it was far too much temptation. He cleared his throat and nodded to her. "Good night, Lizzy."

Standing a few feet above him, they were almost even in height now, and it wouldn't take much for her to lean forward and kiss him. He found himself hoping for that outcome, though he knew it was unlikely.

Instead, her lips just moved into a small smile. "Thank you for showing me the pond, Fitzwilliam. We shall figure out more about our investigation tomorrow morning."

He nodded his agreement and watched her walk up the stairs, conscious of what a fine figure she cut. When she had disappeared from his gaze, he turned to take the other set of stairs that led to his wing of the house.

He was going to wash off before going to bed, and he decided he would not send for his valet to bring him warm water. Instead, he would make do with the cold water that was left from yesterday morning, assuming his valet hadn't emptied the pitcher yet. The basin would of course be empty already. He needed the water to be as cold as possible to help control the shocking thoughts occurring to him.

HE WAITED FOR LIZZY to join him for breakfast the next morning, unsurprised when she slipped down a few minutes past him, though it was still early. They had the breakfast room to themselves, and as she buttered her roll, he said, "I shall go into Lambton to the tavern today and ask about Mr. Terrence's visits there."

"That is an excellent idea. I was going to suggest such a thing myself. Do you suppose we can slip in after dinner, or should we try to visit before?"

He frowned at her. "I shall be going alone, and likely before the dinner hour."

She frowned at him. "You shall likely find looser tongues if you allow them to imbibe a bit longer first, Mr. Darcy. I propose we visit after the meal. We can have tea with the general company, and then I shall excuse myself early. You can leave a short time after me, and we will meet at the carriages."

He scowled at her, speaking firmly. "Your plan is good, except for one oversight."

She seemed annoyed by the possibility, but she opened her eyes wider. "What have I overlooked?"

"A properly bred young woman like yourself will not be going to the tavern with me, Miss Bennet." He deliberately spoke in repressive tones, hoping to shame her for the suggestion.

It didn't work, and she continued to proffer ideas about how she might insert herself into the questioning throughout breakfast, but he was determined to shut down each idea she had. The idea of taking her into the tavern was appalling, and not just for her reputation. She had seen things no fine young woman should have to, and she'd been involved with some sordid business during their acquaintance, but he refused to expose her to such iniquity voluntarily.

She was forced to subside with her wilder and wilder suggestions as Georgiana joined them. Deliberately wanting to keep his sister there, he engaged her in conversation as they discussed what to do about the horses, and what features they would like in the new stables. He invited Lizzy to share her opinion on several occasions, and she seemed surprised by that, but she haltingly offered her viewpoints each time he inquired.

Perhaps she didn't realize it, but he was offering her the opportunity to ensure the stables met her needs as well. She wasn't a horsewoman, but he was determined to make her one after their marriage—and he was clinging to optimism that might still be possible. After all, she'd agreed to come to Pemberley, and she seemed far more open to him than she ever had. She was giving him a second chance, and he intended to make the most of it.

FITZWILLIAM ARRANGED to keep himself busy for the rest of the afternoon mainly so he could avoid another private conversation with Lizzy as she tried to cajole him into accepting her presence at the tavern. Since he was determined that wouldn't happen, it seemed wiser to stay away from her for the afternoon.

Fortunately, there were many duties to which he must attend, including helping plan the new temporary structure and send a missive to the builder who had built his mother's hermitage seventeen years ago. That was the last major renovation that had been done, since smaller tasks could be handled by local tradesmen, but he felt it prudent to have a classically trained architect design the building for them, though he was likely to put local people in charge of building it.

Dinner was more subdued than the night before. Lady Catherine had taken a tray in her room, and Fitzwilliam was happy to have her absent. His aunt was a disapproving and exacting woman, and she was hardly helpful for ensuring good digestion.

After dinner, when Charles started to suggest port, he shook his head. "I have a bit of a headache. I think I shall try a cup of tea to see if it relieves it." Lizzy's suggestion to excuse herself was a good one, and he intended to co-opt that, though he regretted the need to foil her participation. She'd had good ideas about when to approach as well, and he knew it was unfair not to include her, but how could he allow her to enter the tavern with him?

After drinking half of a cup of tea, and watching Lizzy the entire time, he said, "I do believe I shall excuse myself. I have a headache tonight."

"It is likely all the smoke," said Fanny Bennet. "I feel like I am constantly on the verge of tears today, and my nose is dreadfully stuffy."

Apparently, she didn't realize sharing that information was a little indelicate, but Darcy was happy for her remark, and he seized upon it. "No doubt, that is why I have a headache."

Lizzy and Jane both spoke at the same time then, "So do I."

He would have suspected it was some kind of subterfuge, but since Jane had said the words almost at the same time as Lizzy, and Lizzy seemed as surprised as he did, he decided he was being paranoid. "I would not be surprised if we all have some lingering effects of the exposure to all that smoke."

"I have had a dreadful tickle in my chest all day," said Anne.

"Perhaps we should end the evening early," said Lizzy. "I do not know about the rest of you, but I could stand an early night."

The only voice of dissent was Lydia, and she quickly fell silent upon realizing everyone else was in favor of the plan. Darcy admired how Lizzy had maneuvered them all, but he found himself genuinely wondering if she had a headache. His wasn't entirely contrived, and he worried for her health.

Darcy went to his room and waited twenty minutes before going downstairs again. As he walked to the carriage house, having already sent directions to his driver to be waiting for him, he half-expected Lizzy to pop out.

There was no sign of her, and he was almost disappointed that she wasn't trying to maneuver around his embargo of her attendance. It was a strange reaction, though he was certain he had made the right decision by not allowing her to accompany him, but he couldn't pretend he wasn't feeling slightly imbalanced that she wasn't there.

He opened the carriage, once again thoroughly inspecting it, because he almost expected to find Lizzy hiding inside. She wasn't there, and he accepted his disappointment with a strong measure of relief. He didn't want to have to take time to argue with her. Still, he was surprised at her acquiescence.

They were underway soon enough, and as the coach's lantern lit the way ahead of them while Pemberley's lights faded in the distance, he jerked upright when he heard a voice say, "Oi, guvnor, stop."

With a sound of protest from both Darcy's driver and the horses, the carriage suddenly jolted, and the driver brought them to an abrupt halt. "What are you on about, boy?" His driver sounded annoyed, but it changed to outrage when he said, "You cannot do that."

A second later, Darcy realized what *that* was when the door opened, and the young lad clambered inside. He frowned, appalled at the breach of decorum. He was about to dress down the young man when he met his gaze under the oversized top hat and recognized a very fine pair of eyes.

His mouth dropped open in shock, and he was irritated as he said, "How dare you?" Even as he chastised her, he couldn't help admiring both her brazenness in dressing like a boy, and her thought processes leading her to that to start with.

She grinned at him, unrepentant, and he marveled that she had a curly mustache on her lip.

His driver opened the door, clearly working himself into a lather, and Darcy put up a hand. "It is all right, Jensen. The young lad has an injury and requires transport to Lambton. I have agreed."

His driver seemed troubled. "That is most kind of you, Mr. Darcy. The scallywag should have had the decency to at least ask me before climbing into the carriage though." He shot a sour look at Lizzy.

She nodded. "I apologize, Mr. Jensen," she said in a voice that was a few octaves lower than usual. It sounded like it might pain her slightly.

To Darcy, it wasn't at all convincing of a masculine voice, but the driver seemed to notice nothing unusual. No doubt, he saw a young man and was prepared to accept that, especially in his current state of ire. With a mutter under his voice that no one could understand, but Darcy realized was probably not entirely polite, the driver closed the door, and the carriage rocked a moment later as he returned to his seat. Soon, they were underway again.

Once they were, Lizzy moved from the seat across to sit beside him, leaning against him. "Mr. Darcy, thank you for the ride." She fluttered her lashes at him.

It was slightly disconcerting to see the feminine gesture while she was wearing a mustache, and he lifted a finger as he poked at it gingerly. "Where in the world did you get that?"

Lizzy giggled. "I cut about an inch off my hair, and then I stole some gum paste from the kitchen and used it to apply the hair. I do not know how long my mustache will last, but hopefully for the next couple of hours during our endeavor."

He frowned at her severely. "It shall last quite long while you wait in the carriage, I am certain."

She put out her lip and pouted at him. "Come on, Fitzwilliam. Your objection was taking me as a young lady into a tavern. If I am just your servant boy, what is the harm?"

"The harm is, you are trying to manipulate me."

She grinned at him, clearly unabashed. "Is it working?"

He crossed his arms over his chest and glared at her. "No. I shall not risk your safety."

She frowned. "What could happen to me as a young man entering a tavern? I swear I shall not have a single sip of the devil's rum."

"Indeed, you shall not, and you shall not move away from my side. Do you understand?"

Her eyes sparkled. "You concede I may assist you?"

He huffed a sigh, realizing how neatly she had finessed him. "I concede you will likely sneak in right behind me. Short of leaving you tied up in the carriage, I can see no way to foil your determination, so I would prefer to have you in sight and at my side at all times from the beginning."

"Thank you for being so reasonable, Fitzwilliam."

He glared at her. "I do not feel all that reasonable right now, Lizzy."

Her lips twisted into a smile, drawing attention to the strange curly mustache on her face. "Would a kiss bring you into better humor, Mr. Darcy?"

He frowned sternly at her. "I am hardly likely to want to kiss my serving boy."

"Perhaps I can be more than just your serving boy," she said in a teasing tone as she leaned closer, brushing her lips against his cheek. It would have been highly pleasurable, save for the ticklish mustache.

He frowned at her severely as he moved a few inches away. "You shall certainly owe me a kiss when this is over, but I would prefer it without the mustache."

She let out a sigh, looking disappointed as she went back to the seat across him from him. "I did not realize you were such a stickler for propriety, Mr. Darcy."

He scowled. "I hardly think it is being a stickler that I prefer to kiss you when you are not wearing hair on your lip."

She grinned at him then. "Just wait until I am older."

He frowned in confusion. "I do not understand."

Lizzy laughed. "If I inherit my mother's curse, you will if you still know me then."

He was completely mystified by the conversation, and he tried to envision Fanny Bennet using gum paste to stick hair to her upper lip, but it was such a preposterous idea that he found himself laughing instead. He was still annoyed with Lizzy's neat maneuvering of the situation, but it was difficult, if not impossible, to remain irritated with her.

Chapter Five

When Lizzy stepped down, she was startled to feel Fitzwilliam's hands on her hips. Since he had rejected her attempt to kiss him, she was surprised he wanted to touch her in such a fashion until she realized he was simply adjusting her posture.

"Do not walk with such a sway. It is far too effeminate for a young man. You need to walk with your legs slightly apart and your posture looser overall."

Lizzy made an attempt, and the driver let out a shocked sound. "You poor fellow. I did not realize just how injured you were." He seemed to have forgiven him some for his impertinence in entering the carriage.

Lizzy was embarrassed that her male walk had come across as an injury, but she decided to go with it. "Thank you for your concern. I have no doubt a pint of ale will do me wonders." She hoped she'd use the right terminology as she walked behind Mr. Darcy when he moved past her. She was still feeling awkward in her gait, and she was aware of the driver's sympathetic gaze on her as she stumbled in behind him.

She wasn't certain what she'd been expecting, but the dimly lit, smoky room was pretty much in line with it. It was filled with men, and the only woman she saw was the barmaid who was moving among the tables. Mr. Darcy approached the counter, and the barkeep looked up. He grunted at them. "What'll you have?"

"Two ales," said Mr. Darcy.

There was a quiet murmur going through the crowd, and Lizzy realized everyone was staring at them. No doubt, they recognized Mr. Darcy.

He must have decided to go with that, because he turned to the room. "I am here about Mr. Terrence. I know he spent a great deal of time here, so I felt I should break it to his comrades myself. He was killed yesterday."

The murmuring intensified, though Lizzy couldn't tell whether it was more outraged, shocked, or sad.

"I propose we all drink a toast to Mr. Terrence." He turned back to the barkeep. "I would like to provide a round for everyone."

Lizzy admired his tactic, realizing that if he were willing to pay for the alcohol, no doubt, a few loose tongues would be happy to indulge and to the point where they might not remain tightlipped.

Over the next several minutes, she was treated to a side of Fitzwilliam she wouldn't have expected as he took a table, and she sat down beside him, keeping her head down and her hat on to obscure her identity. There was a surprising amount of everyman about him, or at least he was able to adapt to it plausibly, for he settled into conversation with the group.

Mostly, they reminisced about Mr. Terrence, and Lizzy realized most of the people in the room seemed to genuinely like the man. She couldn't be surprised, since he had seemed so warm upon their only meeting.

Mr. Darcy bought three rounds of drinks for everyone, though he and Lizzy weren't drinking, before someone revealed anything that was actually useful. A man beside their table said, "Poor Flora is not going to take the news well."

"Who is Flora?" asked Lizzy in what she hoped was a passably masculine tone.

"She is his favorite at the *Bloom and Petal*," said the man.

Lizzy frowned. "I am not familiar with that establishment."

The man guffawed. "I can hardly be surprised, young man. If you are not old enough to grow your own mustache yet, you are hardly likely to be interested in visiting Madam Childe's establishment."

Lizzy flushed as she realized her mustache hadn't fooled anyone. With a sigh, she lifted a thumbnail and started to peel off the gum paste. "Try as I might, I cannot grow a mustache," she said in her forced-masculine tone.

There were sounds of sympathy for her from a few men, and one of the older ones said, "Do not despair, lad. My son Jackie was a full three-and-twenty before he managed to grow an impressive one."

Lizzy was amazed at the sense of camaraderie, and the sympathy directed toward her. She had imagined men would be sitting around mostly drinking in silence, perhaps exchanging grunts every now and then. She was embarrassed to admit she hadn't considered men had similar emotions to women, having just assumed they didn't feel things as strongly rather than realizing perhaps they had to hide them to conform with society.

"Where might the *Bloom and Petal* be?" asked Mr. Darcy. "I would like to tell this Miss Flora myself."

"Since I am certain you do not know where it is, it is just down the lane and around the corner," said the man who had teased Lizzy about her mustache. He was clearly now jesting about Darcy's professed lack of knowledge of the area. Lizzy found it strange that the master of Pemberley wouldn't understand the layout of Lambton, but she wasn't going to say anything, because she thought maybe there was more going on than she understood.

Fitzwilliam looked briefly offended, but he didn't call the man on his tone or words. Instead, he looked at the barkeep as he laid several more coins on the table. "One more round on me, sir." He stood up, looking at Lizzy and said, "Come on, Benjamin."

She got to her feet, trying to walk with a masculine form, but she heard a few snickers around her that assured her she wasn't successful.

"The poor lad," said one man in a pseudo-whisper. "He cannot grow a mustache or walk straight. No wonder he has no idea where Madam Childe's establishment is."

Lizzy's cheeks burned as the man's words prompted laughter, but she did her best to keep her shoulders stiff as she attempted to make a dignified exit.

When they were out of the tavern, she walked closer beside him, and Darcy said softly, "For goodness sake, it is better to walk like a girl than to walk like that."

She glared up at him as she adjusted her gait to what felt more comfortable, though she still tried not to be too feminine and focused on keeping her hips as immobile as possible. If it was any better, he certainly didn't praise the efforts.

Instead, they walked down the road after Darcy called to his driver that he would return in a while. Lizzy didn't know what exactly they were looking for, but she was searching for a sign that said *Bloom and Petal*, though she saw no such thing. However, there was a discreet sign with a lily on it, and she nudged Mr. Darcy's arm as she pointed to it. "Could that be what we seek?"

He nodded, looking uneasy. "If this establishment is what I think it is, I can see why they do not blatantly advertise. Indeed, I had no idea such a thing existed in Lambton." He seemed vaguely disapproving, which further heightened Lizzy's curiosity.

They moved around back as directed, knocking on the door, which was soon opened by a woman scantily clad in a corset, bustled skirt, and stockings that revealed her leg from mid-thigh down. Lizzy was shocked at the sight, though she did her best to hide it. She stumbled as she crossed the doorway, and the young woman grabbed her arm to prop her up. "First time, gent?"

Lizzy's eyes widened, and she nodded.

"Is your father bringing you?"

Lizzy shook her head. "Mr. Darcy is not my father."

The girl trailed a hand down Lizzy's arm in a way that felt lewd. "While your master is busy, perhaps you would have a few minutes to entertain me?" She winked at Lizzy.

Lizzy's mouth dropped open in shock as she realized what the woman was implying. "I beg your pardon?" Realizing how outraged she sounded, she strove to lower her tone and sound more moderate. "You are not my type, miss." She couldn't help glancing at Darcy as she said that.

The woman's gaze widened, and then she nodded. She looked sympathetic, dropping all hints of flirtation. "I can certainly understand that, lad, but do be careful with your predilections. If the wrong person discovers them, it could mean the noose for you."

Lizzy murmured thanks for her concern, still confused, and the woman turned to an older woman who was speaking with Mr. Darcy. "I do believe I am not needed here, Madam Childe."

The older woman nodded. "You may return to the parlor to entertain our other guests."

Lizzy moved closer, wondering if she'd missed anything of importance during the brief exchange with the young woman. It seemed shocking to her that Mr. Terrence had a preference for spending his time at bawdy houses, but what else could this be?

"What are your interests this evening, Mr. Darcy? I do not believe you have ever graced us with your presence at the establishment before. Surely, you must prefer the delights offered in London?"

Lizzy was amazed at the way Fitzwilliam's cheeks turned ruddy, and he seemed uncomfortable. "I come to deliver bad news."

The madam looked surprised and slightly concerned then. "Surely, you do not plan to shut us down, Mr. Darcy? We have been most discreet, and I am certain you must agree we fulfill a necessary niche—"

He put up a hand. "I do not necessarily approve of your endeavor, but as long as it remains discreet, that is between you and your customers. I simply wanted to speak with Miss Flora."

"I am afraid she is indisposed this evening." The madam looked at her book resting nearby. "The closest I have to someone similar to Flora is Charlene. Would you like to meet her?"

Darcy issued an impatient sigh. "No, Madam, I am here to deliver the news Mr. Terrence has been murdered."

The woman's hands clenched around the book for a moment, and she looked appalled. "Mr. Terrence is dead? Who would want to harm him?"

"I was hoping you or Miss Flora might have some indication." Darcy spoke sternly, as though daring her to deny him the information he sought.

For a moment, she looked defiant, but then her shoulders sagged slightly. "I suppose if you are determined to look into the matter, you will discover at some point that Mr. Terrence owes the *Bloom and Petal* three pounds, eight pence."

Darcy looked thunderstruck. "He owes that much for your services? I did not understand that women in your business extended credit, let alone such an indecent amount."

She shook her head. "He is not indebted for our services. We have a side business, and Mr. Terrence had a taste for roulette. I have extended him credit far too generously, but he is a likable fellow, and he does enjoy his time here. As you can imagine, him owing me that much money is not ideal, but it certainly wouldn't be worth murdering him. After all, how would I collect the debt if he is dead?"

After a moment, Fitzwilliam seemed to accept that, and he nodded grudgingly. "When will I be able to speak with Miss Flora?"

Before the madam could answer, a man stumbled out of the parlor where the young prostitute had disappeared into, and Lizzy gasped at recognizing him. He was too in his cups to be alert enough to realize in whose presence he was for a moment as he stumbled closer to them. He seemed to recognize Fitzwilliam long seconds after Fitzwilliam apparently recognized George Wickham and pulled back his hand.

He punched Wickham in the face, knocking him to the ground as an unconscious lump.

The madam gasped. "Mr. Darcy, you cannot treat my clients this way."

"This man is a wanted thief. You do not want him associated with your establishment, I assure you, Mrs. Childe. Send one of your women to fetch the constable so he can arrest the man."

Lizzy was doing her best to hang back, trying to shield herself from Wickham's gaze by hiding partially behind Fitzwilliam. She didn't want him to recognize her, but fortunately, he seemed too scrambled at the moment to recognize much of anything, though his eyes were starting to open.

That was beginning to change by the time Constable Smith arrived, prompting Wickham to get to his feet and clapping irons around his wrists before marching him ahead of him. Though still dazed, he was more alert now. Lizzy and Darcy followed behind, and Lizzy marveled that the constable had simply arrested Wickham on Darcy's authority without bothering to find out why.

She supposed it must be useful to have that kind of power sometimes, and she recalled how he'd masterfully wielded it against Mr. Collins when he had tried to blackmail Anne. She'd admired it then, and she admired it now. When he used it for good purposes, how could she not?

The four of them entered the constable's office moments later, and Lizzy had been aware of the driver watching it all with curiosity. She wondered what he thought of her changed gait and hopefully dismissed it as a pint having done away with the pain. No doubt, the man was curious as to why she was still following Mr. Darcy, and even more curious why they were entering the constable's office, but he was too well-trained to even ask about when they might be ready to depart, let alone demand to know what they were doing.

Smith pushed Wickham into a chair, not taking him to the cells yet. "What are the charges, Mr. Darcy?"

"This man is wanted for theft in Meryton, along with abduction. Do you receive information about various crimes in other locales?"

"I do, just about once a week. There's a young lad who rides around delivering the weekly wanteds." The older man walked to the desk, quickly sorting through the files there. Everything in the office was spotlessly arranged, and he likely knew exactly what he was looking for. He had to dig through a few piles before finding the one about Wickham, but he returned with it and compared the drawing. "Aye, this is the man. He's also AWOL from the militia."

"All serious allegations. You can add murder to the list," said Fitzwilliam.

Wickham's head snapped up, and he looked at Darcy in shock before his gaze moved to Lizzy. His shock seemed to grow then, and there was a new confidence in his posture when he said, "I do not believe you will be holding me on anything, Mr. Darcy. What do you think, Mr. Bennet?"

Lizzy stiffened at his use of her name, indicating he clearly recognized her. It was an implied threat, she was certain, but she refused to cede to it. "I suspect you will be held accountable for whatever actions you have committed. Did you burn the stables at Pemberley?"

His gaze evaded hers, and it was clear he was lying when he said, "Of course not. Why would I do that? I grew up at Pemberley."

"You did it to vex me," said Darcy. "You have engaged in systemic harassment for the last several weeks when a smart man would have taken advantage of the chance to leave the country entirely."

Wickham seemed to resent the words. "I am quite intelligent. I had the same education as you, Mr. Darcy."

"Indeed you did, yet you chose to squander it. I submit you might be academically intelligent, but you have no common sense."

"What is this charge of murder?" asked Smith, sounding vaguely annoyed. He likely wasn't patient with the derailment.

"This man murdered my stablemaster before setting fire to the stables. He also cut my saddle and tried to kill me weeks ago."

Lizzy frowned, disliking how certain Fitzwilliam sounded. She opened her mouth to tell the constable she wasn't convinced about the stablemaster, but Wickham spoke over her.

He sat up with a new sense of attentiveness, and he appeared entirely earnest when he said, "I have never killed anyone. There was no one in the stables."

She glared at him. "So, you admit to setting the fire?"

After a moment, he nodded sullenly. "I do, but I insist there was no one there. I would have heard them."

"What of the saddle?" asked Darcy.

Wickham looked away but nodded sullenly once. "I had an opportunity and took it. I regretted it later."

As Darcy snorted at the claim, Lizzy continued the conversation about the stablemaster. "You would have known if someone was there even if they were already dead before you started the fire? Did you venture into all the depths of the stables, Mr. Wickham?" asked Lizzy briskly.

He looked down for a moment, shaking his head. "I did not see the need. There was plenty of hay toward the front, along with that big pile of straw. They seemed perfectly adequate for my needs." He appeared annoyed with them when he said, "I did not want the horses to be injured. I wanted you to have plenty of time to get them out first."

Fitzwilliam sneered, clearly disbelieving him, but Lizzy wasn't entirely certain Darcy was maintaining an open enough mind. While she doubted there was little Wickham would not do, he seemed genuinely angered that they thought he might want to injure the horses, and he had been appalled at the accusation of murder.

"There is a Runner *en route* from London, and I shall send him to you as soon as he arrives, Constable Smith. In the meantime, keep this man locked up. Your continued position in Lambton depends on your ability to do so."

The older man swallowed thickly, but he nodded. "No one has ever escaped my cell, I assure you, Mr. Darcy."

Lizzy wanted to ask if anyone had ever tried, but she decided not to provoke him or add to the tenseness of the situation. She really wanted to be alone with Fitzwilliam to discuss the situation.

They left the constable's office moments later, and Lizzy did her best to walk sedately beside him as they went back to the carriage. If the driver considered it odd that Mr. Darcy was allowing the urchin to ride along, he didn't say anything this time. He just shot her a look of disapproval as she opened the door for Mr. Darcy before climbing in behind him. It was a little more awkward without someone to assist her, but she appreciated the freedom the clothing allowed. She'd heard things tonight and learned of different events she never would have dressed as Lizzy Bennet.

Mr. Darcy didn't speak for a few minutes until they were away from Lambton. "I knew it was him."

"He most certainly has been harassing you and set the fire in the stables, but I am not convinced he is the murderer."

Chapter Six

Fitzwilliam's mouth dropped open at her assertion, and he could hardly credit it for a moment. "You do not believe he is the murderer? I was willing to possibly entertain the idea when there was no proof he was the one setting the fire and doing the other acts, but having admitted to those, I have no doubt he was the one who killed Mr. Terrence."

"It is just that he seemed so insistent he did not. I still maintain that perhaps he might kill someone in a cowardly fashion, but I do not believe he would have done so in such a direct manner."

He scowled at her, appalled she didn't support his conclusion. "I submit the man would do anything to survive, and if he were setting the fire and was caught by Mr. Terrence, who confronted him, he might have done anything at that moment to avoid being captured. After all, he faces the noose or deportation to Australia."

She nodded. "I understand that, but he seemed genuinely surprised to learn there was a dead person in the stables. I find it almost impossible to believe Mr. Wickham did that murder."

While he normally admired her quick mind, he was suspicious of it this time. "It is almost as if you are searching for a way to exonerate him from such a foul action. Could it be you still bear affection for the man?"

Lizzy's arms crossed over her chest as she glared at him. "I have no affection for Wickham, but nor do I want to see an innocent man hang."

He snorted. "George Wickham is the very farthest thing from innocent, I assure you. Have you forgotten his actions in Meryton? How he kidnapped Georgiana? Or how he tried to seduce her the year before? These are not the actions of an innocent man."

She had the good grace to flush and look away for a moment before she nodded as her gaze returned to his. "I agree I used the wrong word, but I do not believe he is necessarily a murderer."

"Normally, I trust your judgment, but it is clearly clouded on this issue."

She glared at him. "I could say the same about you, Mr. Darcy."

He pressed on, ignoring her interruption. "When Mr. Kenton arrives, I shall speak with him and direct him toward Constable Smith. They shall take over the investigation, but it is clear to me I cannot trust your input on the matter. Your role in determining what happened to Mr. Terrence is over. Are we clear, Miss Bennet?"

Her arms were still over her chest, and she was glaring at him heatedly. "You do not have the power to deny me a role in the investigation, Mr. Darcy."

He scowled at her. "Do I not? All I have to do is tell your mother the visit is terminated, and you are returning to Longbourn. That will end your interference."

She looked betrayed for a moment, and as though she was having a difficult time drawing a deep breath. "That is not all it would end, Mr. Darcy." With those words, she turned away from him, staring out into the darkness of the night, though the curtain on the window prevented her from seeing anything.

Darcy settled back in his seat, recognizing the truth of her words. How could he allow her to continue to interfere when she was determined Wickham wasn't guilty though? He still wasn't convinced her judgment wasn't clouded for reasons she didn't want to admit, and that added jealousy to his already existing anger. He was disinclined to break the silence either, and they completed the rest of the ride to Pemberley without speaking.

When they arrived, Lizzy stepped down and rushed away into the darkness, and he assumed she was planning to enter through the servants' quarters to return to her room. If he hadn't been so irritated with her, he would have insisted on seeing her up, or at least to her stairs, but there seemed little risk now that the murderer was secured in Constable Smith's cell.

Chapter Seven

Perhaps it was because of the early night, but everyone was down for breakfast earlier than usual the next morning. Lizzy was relieved by that, because it meant she wouldn't have to share a nearly silent meal with Fitzwilliam. She had calmed down considerably throughout the night as she stewed over the situation, and while she understood his viewpoint, she couldn't condone his implication of murder without evidence.

She didn't truly believe he planned to send her away either. He was acting out of the misguided belief she had some sympathy or unwarranted emotion for Wickham. Knowing he had a history of jealous behavior explained some of his reaction, though it didn't excuse the threat. He had done some harm to the progress they were making, but she wasn't ready to swan off to Longbourn and forget all about how she felt for the stubborn man.

Realizing she would have preferred a quiet breakfast with him alone, so they could talk about it more, she was soon disgruntled with everyone around the table. Not every person was there though, and she realized Caroline Bingley hadn't arrived yet.

As though thinking about her had summoned her, the redhead entered the room a moment later, carrying a worn jacket. Lizzy recognized it immediately, for she had purloined it from the laundry room in the basement yesterday afternoon, along with the rest of the attire she had stolen to make herself into Mr. Bennet.

She was hardly surprised when Caroline held it aloft and looked at Lizzy in an accusing fashion. She sounded far too pleased with herself when she said, "Last night, I heard Miss Bennet's door open late, so I looked out to see what was happening, and I saw a young man slip into her room."

There were gasps of outrage, a few words of protest, and a delighted laugh from Lady Catherine. Lizzy herself groaned at the situation, realizing she was going to have to admit what she had done. Only Mr. Darcy remained silent, and she wanted to look to him for solidarity, but she wasn't sure she could count on that after the exchange the evening before.

"How do you explain this?" demanded Lady Catherine. She was practically gleeful, clearly believing this would put heed to any attempt her nephew might make to woo Lizzy.

Lizzy gave her a calm look before turning to Caroline. "You are most observant, Miss Caroline. You did in fact see a man come into my room last night."

Caroline's mouth dropped open for a moment, as though she were shocked Lizzy was blatantly admitting it. "I suppose you have some innocent explanation?" Her voice dripped with doubt.

"Indeed, I do, for I was that man."

There was stark silence for a moment followed by more whispered conversation as she stood up and walked over to Caroline. Calmly, she extracted the jacket from the woman's hands and slipped it on. "It is not a perfect fit without a tailor, of course, but it was passably good enough to convince the fine folks of Lambton."

Mostly, there was just stunned silence dominating, but Jane asked, "What did you do, Lizzy?"

"I believe there is more to Mr. Terrence's death than dying in a fire. If you have not heard it yet, the poor man was stabbed likely before the fire ever occurred. I wanted to know more about him, and to learn who might wish him harm, so I dressed up as a young man and went into Lambton to talk to the men at the tavern."

She was aware of how inappropriate that was, but it was still far preferable to having been caught with a lover in her room.

Caroline seized on this. "What a bold lie. What woman would do that? You are clearly trying to invent such an outrageous falsehood so we will not focus on the truth, which is some man graced your bed last night." She flushed as she said that, sending an apologetic look to her brother. "Pardon my language, Charles."

Mr. Bingley was frowning, and he didn't bother to respond.

Lizzy tensed when Darcy cleared his throat then. "She is not lying, Miss Caroline."

The color drained rapidly from Caroline's face as she looked at Darcy. Clearly, she wanted to accuse him of lying for Lizzy, but she had better sense than to do so. Likely, she also realized there was little chance Fitzwilliam would have colluded with Lizzy after the fact. "How do you know?" There was still a hint of accusation in her tone.

Fitzwilliam's shoulders stiffened, and he gave her a glare. "I know, because I was with Miss Bennet. She dressed as my serving boy, and I escorted her into the tavern to ensure her safety."

Caroline was still clearly shocked, but then she smiled. "Surely, aware of her peculiarities, you cannot seriously be regarding Miss Eliza in any fashion now?"

"My opinion and feelings for Miss Bennet are unchanged," he said in a foreboding way that dared Caroline to keep picking at the topic.

Caroline didn't dare, but Lady Catherine rushed in. "Surely, you cannot condone such actions as for her to be traipsing around dressed like a man, in the company of other men?"

"It was necessary for the situation, and that is all you need to know, Lady Catherine. I sanctioned her activities, and it is a nonissue." He looked to Caroline again. "I do thank you for looking after my interests, Miss Caroline, but I assure you it is entirely unnecessary."

Caroline looked severely deflated when she sank into the empty seat at the table waiting for her.

Feeling buoyed in spite of their argument the night before, Lizzy carefully removed the jacket and handed it to a footman who was standing at the doorway. "If you could see that is returned to the laundry room, I would be most appreciative."

The young man was agog, but he was doing his best to hide that behind a bland expression. "Yes, Miss Bennet," he said softly as he nodded his head. With a nod from the butler, he quickly disappeared to carry out the task.

Lizzy returned to her chair, trying to seem calmer than she felt. The whole incident could have been far uglier, but when she met her aunt's gaze across the table, she was surprised to see Aunt Gardiner was smiling. She seemed almost intrigued by the process, and Lizzy had no doubt her aunt would want to know all about the adventure later.

Her mother, on the other hand, seemed on the verge of collapse. She was fanning herself rapidly with her fan, and Lizzy was afraid the bones might break and fly off to impale someone.

"Elizabeth Bennet, never in my life... How could you... Well, I just cannot imagine." With those words, she fanned herself briskly for another minute before returning her attention to a cup of tea that she drank in several long gulps, apparently needing to fortify herself.

Then, she introduced the topic of the wainscoting in the breakfast room, ruminating on it with much enthusiasm. Though Fitzwilliam was clearly amused, his lips twitching, he indulged the conversation, and by the time breakfast was over, Lizzy had learned all about the history of wainscoting throughout Pemberley, who had provided each work of art, and exactly how much it had cost at her mother's impudent insistence. She was thoroughly sick of the topic, but at least it had drawn away from interrogation about her actions.

AFTER BREAKFAST, LIZZY lingered in the dining room. Caroline seemed determined to wait her out, likely wanting to prevent her from spending any time with Mr. Darcy, but her goal was thwarted when Fitzwilliam approached to ask Lizzy if she wanted to go for a walk. She nodded, and the way he had phrased it, directed toward her, made it clear even to Caroline Bingley that she wasn't included in the invitation. With a huffing sound, she got up from the table and strode from the breakfast room, making no attempt to hide her irritation.

Fitzwilliam took Lizzy's arm with his, and they started walking, not speaking until they were away from the house. "I am sorry I spoke so harshly to you last night," said Fitzwilliam.

Lizzy sighed. "I concede why you might think that, but I assure you I am not sympathetic toward Wickham, or blind to his faults." She could point out that perhaps if either one of them were blinded, it was Fitzwilliam, but they were trying to restore peace, and she had no interest in continuing the strife.

"I firmly believe Wickham was the one who killed Mr. Terrence along with all the other acts of terror in which he has engaged."

Lizzy nodded. "I know." There was little point in reiterating she didn't necessarily believe that. He knew where her thoughts lay on the matter, and there would be nothing gained by continuing to argue about it unless she had proof Wickham was innocent of at least the one act.

"Truthfully, I am happy to hand it all over to Constable Smith and Mr. Kenton. I am certain you agree Mr. Kenton is competent, and if there is any doubt about my version of events, he will uncover it."

Lizzy was poised to argue for a moment, but she just accepted with a sigh and a nod. She had no intention of completely abandoning the investigation, because though Mr. Kenton seemed quite competent, she wasn't sure he couldn't be swayed by Mr. Darcy's dogmatic charisma and conviction of Wickham's character and actions.

She had no sympathy for Wickham, but she couldn't stand by and let him hang if he truly hadn't killed Mr. Terrence. Not only would it be unfair to Wickham, though that didn't bother her too much, but it would be extremely unfair to Mr. Terrence to deny him the justice he deserved by identifying who had actually murdered him.

They paused near a hill, and she looked down as she admired the panorama around them. "Pemberley really is a lovely place, Fitzwilliam."

"It is not as lovely as you."

His tender tone caught her attention, and she turned to look at him. He was staring at her intently, and though there were still rancor remaining from their disagreement about Wickham and the crime, she softened toward him immediately. They could disagree about one thing and still try to be building toward a future together. With that in mind, she gave him a small smile. "I do believe I owe you a kiss, without the mustache."

He nodded, looking solemn. "That is true. I would very much like to collect on it if you are ready, Miss Bennet?"

"I was ready last night, even when wearing the mustache."

He bent his head, his lips taking hers, and they shared a gentle kiss that lasted for a few minutes. When he pulled away, she said, "I must concede, it is more pleasant without the mustache."

"I concur with that viewpoint." He looked like he might kiss her again for a moment, but instead, with a regretful sigh, he put space between them, tucking her hand onto his arm as they returned to Pemberley.

Chapter Eight

Lizzy was happy to have peace back between them, but her mind kept gnawing at the quandary of who had killed Mr. Terrence, and she was determined to speak with Flora, the one person they had not yet had a chance to interview. Knowing the Runner was due to arrive sometime that morning, Lizzy rose even earlier than usual, dressed quickly, and commandeered the phaeton and a driver to take her into Lambton.

Fortunately, it was a different driver than the one who'd experienced her humiliation as Mr. Bennet, though she didn't know if he would have recognized her in a proper walking dress. She had him park roughly where Fitzwilliam's driver had stopped the other evening, and after the driver had assisted her to step down, she said, "I shall return presently."

He looked like he wanted to object, because Lizzy had come alone. She hadn't brought an abigail with her, or any other sort of escort. He was too well-trained to protest, and Lizzy strolled sedately down the street until she was out of his sight.

She rounded the corner to find the *Bloom and Petal*, and she hastened her speed considerably. It wouldn't do to be seen entering or exiting the bawdy house, particularly when she was dressed as Lizzy Bennet. Moments later, she was knocking on the back door. It was considerably early, especially since the women working inside likely kept late hours, so Lizzy had to knock several times before the door finally opened.

She was confronted with Doris Childe, who looked a little grumpy, but sounded mostly amused when she said, "If your man is here, he shall return home after he sleeps it off." She started to close the door.

Lizzy put out a hand. "I am not here about my man. I would like to speak with you and Miss Flora."

Madam Childe stared at her for a moment, and then her lips twitched. "Are you not Mr. Bennet, who was in the accompaniment of Mr. Darcy the other evening?"

Lizzy flushed a little, but she nodded. "I thought you might be more direct with me if I were forthcoming about my true identity."

Looking intrigued, Doris stepped aside to allow her to enter. "May I offer you tea?"

Lizzy nodded her acceptance, waiting in the sitting room where Doris directed her. When Doris came in with a tray moments later, Lizzy wondered if she had brewed it herself. Surely, they must have servants at the bawdy house, but perhaps she didn't want to wake them out of consideration, or maybe she was anxious to keep Lizzy's visit hidden as well.

Lizzy took the cup of tea from her and sipped it appreciatively. "This is lovely."

"Thank you. One of my suitors is a spice importer from China, and he acquires a special blend for me."

Lizzy wondered what a *suitor* was to the woman, but she didn't bother to pry. Instead, she said, "We never did get a chance to speak with Miss Flora, and I would like to talk to her about Mr. Terrence."

The other woman looked troubled. "I do not know what Miss Flora could tell you about Mr. Terrence."

"By all accounts, she knew him well. I would like to get to the bottom of the situation before the Runner becomes involved. Mr. Darcy will be telling him everything we have learned, so he shall likely be knocking on your door next."

The madam looked briefly irritated, but then she sighed. "Yes, I suppose that is true. I confess, I would rather assist you to solve the mystery."

"Do you fear the Runner?" asked Lizzy with genuine curiosity. She wasn't certain of the legality of Madam Childe's establishment.

"Not overly much. In truth, it would be quite satisfying to assist another woman with solving the mystery. No doubt, they will wrest the victory from you in some fashion, but we would know the facts."

Lizzy grinned at her, feeling an unexpected solidarity with the woman. "Indeed, that is my view as well."

"In that case, I shall arrange for you to see Flora. You understand you shall have to pay her normal visiting fee?"

Lizzy had her pin money in her reticule, though she wasn't certain how much to expect. When Doris named the price, she thought about grumbling, but she had enough to cover the expense. If Mr. Terrence was routinely paying this fee, he must have had a particular regard for the woman.

"Come with me, Miss Bennet, and I shall retrieve Flora for you."

Lizzy followed her up the stairs, surprised by how immaculately kept the environment was. Had she ever envisioned herself inside a bawdy house, she would have expected it to be far more lurid than this.

Expectation met reality when Madam Childe showed her into a room moments later. It was a ridiculously frilly bedroom, and there was obviously only one purpose for it. Lizzy was careful not to sit down anywhere or touch anything, not wanting to contemplate what might remain on the surfaces. She contented herself with standing, counting down the moments until Flora finally joined her.

She stiffened when the doorknob turned, and a thin, sallow woman entered seconds later. She was closer to Fanny's age than Lizzy's, and she looked as though life had given her a series of difficulties. There was something frail about her, and Lizzy regretted the need to question her.

Flora seemed surprised to see her, and after a moment, she assumed a seductive expression. "I do not often have ladies visit me. I assure you, I am skilled in all the Eastern arts, and you shall enjoy your visit."

Lizzy wasn't entirely certain what she was getting at, but she thought it had something to do with the house's primary function. She shook her head quickly. "I am not here for that, Miss Flora. I wanted to know more about Mr. Terrence."

The seductive smile fled, and the woman looked haunted for a moment before her lids drooped, partially shielding her gaze. "I had heard he died."

"He was murdered," said Lizzy gently.

Flora flinched at the words, and she drew her shawl tighter about her. "It is a tragedy."

"How frequently did Mr. Terrence visit you?"

"Many times per week," said Flora after a moment. "He started asking exclusively for me." There was a note of pride in her tone, and there was something else in her expression. Lizzy wasn't certain what she would call it, but perhaps fondness and affection. Maybe even something stronger.

"Did you welcome Mr. Terrence's attentions?"

Flora squared her shoulders. "He was a kind man, compassionate and decent. He never treated me like I was lesser for what I do."

"He does sound like he was a good man. Can you think of anyone who might have wanted to cause him harm?"

Flora's reaction was unexpected. She burst into tears and rushed from the room. Lizzy went after her, calling, "Miss Flora, please come back," but the woman entered another room farther down the hall and slammed the door. Lizzy was walking toward it, uncertain what to do, when Madam Childe reappeared.

"I am afraid Flora is too upset to speak with you today. When she is feeling better, I shall arrange another meeting, but I shall ask you to leave her to her grief now."

Lizzy wanted to argue, but it seemed unlikely she was going to get anything from Flora in her current state. "She mentioned Mr. Terrence visited frequently. How frequently would that be?"

The madam hesitated for a moment before she said, "I suspect there were times when he was visiting us that he should have been on duty, so I did not say that to Mr. Darcy. I did not wish to tarnish his impression of Mr. Terrence, who was a good man, despite his love of roulette. He favored Flora with much of his attention, and we all liked him here."

Doris looked regretful. "I wish we could be of more assistance, and I will certainly see to it that Miss Flora meets you when she is up for it, but I do not think you will find your answers here. I cannot think of anyone in this establishment who bore ill will toward Mr. Terrence."

Lizzy accepted her words with a sigh, believing Doris was likely correct. There had to be something she was missing, but she didn't think she would find it at the bawdy house. Perhaps Miss Flora could still give her a clue where to look though, and she maintained interest in speaking with her as she parted from the *Bloom and Petal* moments later.

Lizzy rounded the corner and was walking sedately again when she saw Mr. Darcy standing outside the constable's office with Mr. Kenton. It wasn't at all dignified, but she made a mad dash for the phaeton and was climbing up when a hand wrapped around her wrist moments later. She froze at a disapproving sound before Mr. Darcy said, "How unexpected to see you here, Miss Bennet."

Chapter Nine

Darcy could hardly credit it when he saw Lizzy coming up the street. Based purely on the direction from which she came, he had a strong suspicion where she had been. He excused himself from Mr. Kenton rather abruptly and hurried to his phaeton, having been too engrossed with bringing the Runner to meet the constable to realize it belonged to Pemberley upon their arrival moments before.

The wily Miss Bennet almost escaped him, but he clamped his hand around her wrist and gently tugged her down to join him on the ground. "What are you doing here, Lizzy?"

She gave him a bright smile. "I was simply out for a walk, Fitzwilliam. It is a fine day for it, is it not?"

Despite his irritation, he couldn't suppress a little amusement at the way she was trying to bluff her way through. "It is indeed a fine day, but as you generally confine your walks to Pemberley, I fail to see why you needed to rise so early, steal a phaeton from the carriage house, commandeer a driver to bring you into Lambton, and all so you could just walk around in the town."

"A change of scenery might change one's perspective?" She seemed to be trying to sound confident about that, but there was definitely a note of uncertainty.

Darcy looked at his driver, nodding. "You may return to Pemberley, Stelwarth. I shall see Miss Elizabeth home in my carriage."

The driver touched his hat. "Very good, sir." With a nod for Lizzy, he was soon negotiating the phaeton out of the space it had occupied and returning to Pemberley.

Lizzy seemed outraged. "That was my return to Pemberley."

"You shall ride with me."

She gasped. "There is no escort, and I am dressed as me."

"Your reputation would be far more tattered if anyone else had seen you enter and leave the establishment where you just visited." He crossed his arms over his chest. "Deny it."

She licked her lips, appearing nervous, but then she straightened her shoulders. "I have nothing to deny. I simply met with Miss Flora. I must tell you about my interview with her."

He prodded her toward the carriage. "You may speak freely on the ride back to Pemberley."

She looked vaguely resentful for a moment, but she stepped into the carriage without protest when he handed her up before following. He waited to speak until they had left the vicinity of Lambton, and then he scowled at her. "Do you have any idea how irresponsible and reckless it was for a woman like you to enter Madam Childe's establishment?"

Lizzy frowned at him. "I am aware the scandal it would cause, which is why I picked my arrival to be so early, certain to avoid anyone seeing."

"And perhaps to move in before the Runner had a chance to interrogate the women at the bawdy house?" He arched a brow as he expected her denial.

She surprised him by nodding. "There is that too. You have forbidden me to investigate, but I do not respond well to edicts, Mr. Darcy. Frankly, I am surprised you do not know that about me by now."

He was still irritated at her actions, but most of his ire had drained away. "I do not like you putting yourself at risk for this. Allow Mr. Kenton to prove Mr. Wickham's guilt."

Lizzy frowned at him. "I am still not convinced Mr. Wickham killed Mr. Terrence."

He scowled. "Are we back to this again? I do not trust your judgment in the matter."

"Nor did I trust your judgment when it came to my sister Jane, but you were wrong, were you not? I am willing to concede there is a possibility I am wrong as well, but to discard any other option because of your bias toward Wickham is not a balanced way to investigate."

He opened his mouth to protest, but his anger from the evening when she had seemed to be defending Wickham had cooled over the intervening days, and while he was still annoyed she didn't accept his word on it, he no longer believed she was acting out of some lingering affection for the rogue. "If it was not Wickham, who else would it be?"

Lizzy seemed stunned by his words for a moment, and then she smiled brightly. "I have no idea, but I suggest we search his things. The groom said he had been sleeping in the quarters off the tack room of late as an extra security precaution, but that must mean he has apartments elsewhere?"

Darcy nodded. "There is a housing structure near the stables for the employees."

"As soon as we get back to Pemberley, we must thoroughly examine his belongings."

Fitzwilliam frowned at the idea. "If we are seen entering his quarters alone, it will cause gossip."

"Can it be any more gossip-inspiring than me dressing up as a boy, and you sanctioning it?" she asked with a sparkle in her eyes.

He frowned at her severely. "I did not sanction it."

Lizzy seemed undeterred. "Yet you implied you did when you spoke with Miss Bingley after she forced the confrontation in front of everyone. What am I to think, Mr. Darcy? After all, you did allow me to accompany you for the price of a kiss."

Recognizing the opening, though he wasn't certain if Lizzy had given it by design, he said, "I do find you are able to persuade me to do an alarming number of things with a simple kiss."

She crossed the carriage to sit beside him. "In that case, perhaps I could convince you to assist me with searching Mr. Terrence's apartment?" As she asked, she brought her mouth ever closer, until the last word made her lips brush against his cheek. Then she kissed it lightly.

With a chuckle, he put his arm around her shoulders and pulled her closer. "That is hardly a kiss."

She looked up at him, eyes wide and lips parted. He groaned aloud when she licked the plump contours in a suggestive fashion. "Perhaps you should demonstrate what you consider a kiss then, Fitzwilliam?"

He bent his head and spent the next few minutes doing just that, before realizing he was far too close to losing control. With strength he didn't know he had, he gently pushed her way and nudged her to return to the seat across from him. He needed the distance between them to maintain propriety.

With her cheeks flushed, eyes shining, and lips swollen from his kisses, she'd never looked lovelier. He bunched his gloved hands into fists at his side and mentally recited rules of geometry until he felt more in command.

Lizzy had been content with the silence, and his brain hadn't been functioning well enough to fill it with conversation. Now there was no chance, since they'd arrived at Pemberley. As soon as the carriage drew to a halt, Lizzy bounded out without assistance, and Darcy followed behind her, understanding she was inspired by the new lead, but wishing she had at least waited for him.

She was the very antithesis of discreet as she charged across the grounds, heading toward the building she had correctly surmised housed the servants' apartments. At least she waited for him to catch up with her then, and he frowned down at her. "We could have walked together."

She was clearly too impatient for that. "Which apartment belongs to Mr. Terrence?"

"As the stablemaster, he is entitled to have his own separate quarters, so his apartment is on the bottom." He led her in the proper direction after taking her hand and placing it on his arm. He insisted they walk with dignity, should they be under observation.

He had no doubt someone was awake and watching, and it would likely be all over Pemberley lands by the evening that he and Lizzy had visited Mr. Terrence's apartment together alone, but it couldn't be helped. At most, it would create the kind of pressure that dictated they marry to avoid scandal. He would prefer to have her assent under other terms, but he wasn't too proud to admit he would take her under that scenario as well, if she weren't too stubborn to accept.

Mr. Terrence's rooms were unlocked, and they walked in seconds later. Fitzwilliam couldn't deny he felt out of place poking through the dead man's things. If Lizzy felt any such hesitation, it didn't impede her attempts, and she was soon searching through his nooks and crannies.

Fortifying himself, Fitzwilliam moved to the escritoire and began searching for any clues through the man's correspondences. Other than his inkwell being slightly untidy with drops of ink, there was nothing out of place, and nothing that stood out as suspicious.

He stood up at Lizzy's grunt, frowning at her. "Is something wrong?"

She shook her head, looking impatient. "No, I suppose I am just frustrated. I did not expect a handwritten confession from the killer, but I was hoping for more information." She waved a hand. "Other than his taste for roulette and bawdy houses, Mr. Terrence appears to have led a quiet life."

Mr. Darcy nodded his agreement, and trying to cheer her, he said, "There is still his bedroom to search. Perhaps we might find something there."

Lizzy nodded as she followed him into that room, going straight to the nightstand. Fitzwilliam felt even more uncomfortable to be searching this area, but it needed to be done, so he stiffened his spine and went to the dresser. He started sorting through the various items of clothing there, but he saw nothing of interest. He was prepared to consider the whole endeavor a waste of time when Lizzy let out a sound that was close to, "Aha."

He turned from the dresser and faced her. "What is it?"

She held a silver box in her hand, and as he moved closer, he realized she'd already opened the hinged compartment, revealing a sapphire and silver ring inside. He saw nothing remarkable about it. "What is it?"

"It is an expensive gift. It does not seem like the kind of trinket a man of Mr. Terrence's salary could easily afford to give. Rather, it seems like the kind of token a man might bestow when proposing to someone."

That piqued his interest, and he took the box from her to examine the ring more closely. The diamond chips were small and not as clear as pieces he had seen in his mother's and sister's collections, and the sapphire could have been bigger, but he could see it would be an expensive piece for a man of Mr. Terrence's income. "I believe your theory is sound, but who was he courting and prepared to marry?"

Lizzy gave him an impish grin. "You never did give me a chance to tell you about my interview with Miss Flora."

He frowned in shock. "You believe he bought this for a lady of the evening?"

Lizzy shrugged a shoulder. "Flora was his favorite, and he was visiting more frequently than Madam Childe led us to believe. When I asked if she knew of anyone who might want to harm him, Flora burst into tears and ran from the room. She was clearly a woman grieving."

Something in her tone alerted Fitzwilliam. "But?"

After a moment, she shrugged. "Perhaps she was more than just grieving. I would very much like to speak with her again. Madam Childe assured me she would contact me when Flora was up to another interview, but I believe you might have more luck in pressing the issue. I think it would be prudent to speak to her sooner rather than later."

Seeing the wisdom of her suggestion, he said, "I shall send a missive along with a persuasive amount to ensure Madam Childe will arrange an interview with Flora as quickly as possible."

Lizzy came over, tucking her arm through his and giving him a side-hug. "It must be terribly effective to wield the kind of power you do, Mr. Darcy. Have I mentioned to you how much I admire that you do not abuse it?"

His face heated at the compliment, and he felt unexpectedly shy. He quelled the urge to look away from her and forced an indulgent smile. "I have already capitulated to your plan. There is no reason to oversell your point."

She sniffed at him, but she still appeared amused. "The gracious way to accept a compliment is with a thank you, Mr. Darcy. I am surprised a man of your income, likely instructed by the finest governesses, and with normally exquisite manners, does not know that."

Lips twitching, he led her from Mr. Terrence's apartment, pausing when they had stepped outside to say, "Thank you."

Chapter Ten

After a brief walk with Fitzwilliam, Lizzy returned to her room at Pemberley, eagerly awaiting word from Fitzwilliam after he had arranged the meeting, though she knew it could even be tomorrow before Madam Childe could make it happen. She couldn't deny Flora had been upset, but she wasn't certain if it was a reasonable degree of reaction, or if there had been more than loss prompting her response.

Lizzy carefully tucked the silver box into her nightstand, thinking it might serve another purpose yet. As she did so, she saw a note sitting atop the furniture, and she lifted the piece of paper.

Reading quickly, Lizzy surmised Anne wanted to meet her at the cottage where she had met with Carlos the other day. There was a frantic tone to the note, and Lizzy was alarmed, especially since it directed her to come as soon as possible.

It was only a little past her normal hours for rising, thanks to her unusually early start, so she dared hope Anne hadn't left the missive much earlier. Likely, she'd come to Lizzy's room, and upon finding her not there, she had availed herself of the escritoire to leave the message.

Feeling alarmed, Lizzy left her room and then Pemberley moments later, slipping out through the servants' entrance, since it put her closer to the cottage. She ignored the surprised look of the two footmen she passed along the way, breaking into a run as soon as she was far enough from Pemberley that she didn't have to worry too much about her dignity.

Lizzy burst into the cottage moments later, expecting to see Anne. Instead, she heard something scraping across the porch seconds after entering, and she realized someone had blocked the door when she tried the doorknob reflexively. She turned and pounded on it, calling, "I am in here. Open the door."

Receiving no response, and truthfully not having expected one, Lizzy turned from the door after attempting to push it open several times. The doorknob wouldn't budge, and she closed her eyes for a moment, trying to visualize the porch as it had been when she approached.

There had been a chair there, a sturdy one she didn't recall seeing the first time she and Anne had found the location, or when she had escorted her friend to visit Carlos. As she visualized it in her mind, it didn't seem like it was coated with dust, and it was a finer quality than should be at this basic cottage. Someone had likely carried it from Pemberley, planning just this deed.

Lizzy was uneasy about their intentions, and as her imagination ran away with her, she could picture someone throwing a torch through the window, though she couldn't imagine who hated her enough to kill her.

A groan distracted her, and she moved deeper into the room, realizing there was a form on the bed. She rushed toward it, startled to find Carlos sprawled there. She'd heard him groan, so she knew he was alive, but she still touched her fingers to his neck, ensuring his pulse was steady underneath it. She shook his shoulder. "Carlos, wake up."

There was no response, so she shook harder. Even when she clapped her hands inches from his face, there was no effect, leading her to conclude someone had drugged him, likely with laudanum. Had they done the deed elsewhere, or had they lured him here, anticipating a meeting with Anne?

Lizzy moved away from him, two purposes in mind. She was hoping for a second exit, though she soon discovered the small cottage didn't have one, and she was also looking for other evidence to explain what might have happened here. In the kitchen, she found a partially eaten cheese board and an open bottle of wine with two glasses. There was a note on the floor, and she bent to pick it up, taking it to the nearest window, because it was too gloomy in the room to read otherwise.

It was a risqué note, ostensibly penned by Anne. It suggested Carlos have a glass of wine to relax while he waited for Anne join him, for she had a surprise he would greatly enjoy.

Carlos had been neatly maneuvered to arrive and drink the wine while he waited for his lover. She wondered if he had drunk the wine last night or this morning. If he was still drugged from last night, whoever had given him the dose had risked killing him.

She walked around the cottage again, eyeing the windows, and dissatisfied that none of them would offer easy exit. They were all small and high, and there weren't that many to start with. A few minutes later, she froze at the scraping sound, recognizing it was the chair being moved. Lizzy started to rush for the door, but she hesitated. She wasn't certain exactly what was happening, but she doubted someone was rescuing her.

That impression changed a moment later when Fitzwilliam swept into the cottage, a fierce frown on his face. She wanted to throw herself at him in relief, and she would have if Caroline Bingley hadn't entered directly behind him, followed by Lady Catherine. Miss Anne was trailing behind, looking fretful.

"I told you what I saw. Do you believe me now, Mr. Darcy?" There was a note of victory in Caroline's tone as she pointed to Lizzy, and then Carlos's form slumped on the bed. "She is meeting with the groom."

Anne let out a gasp, and Lizzy met her gaze, trying to relay with her eyes that Caroline was lying. She was relieved to see Anne looked upset, but she didn't appear angry with Lizzy. She seemed disbelieving of the setup.

"Surely this madness must end now," said Lady Catherine. "You are bringing disgrace to our name to even entertain the possibility of taking this hoyden as your wife. She is a wanton, and she has no regard for propriety or the classes."

"I received a note penned by someone else that suggested a different purpose to this meeting entirely, Lady Catherine. It was to be a lead on Mr. Terrence's death." She quickly invented that idea, seeing how Caroline's eyes widened with surprise. She had little doubt who had penned the notes to both her and Carlos, for they were in the same hand. "Instead, someone locked me in here, and I found Carlos drugged on the bed."

Lady Catherine let out a sound of outrage. "You call him by his first name, so you must have been intimate."

"I simply bothered to learn his name, Lady Catherine." Lizzy walked over to the bed, lifting Carlos's hand. She held it aloft for a moment, and it dropped immediately to the mattress as soon as she released it. "He is oblivious."

Anne rushed forward then, bending down to feel Carlos's neck as Lizzy had done moments before. She sounded relieved when she said, "He is alive."

Lizzy nodded. "I do not think anyone wants to kill him, though if they drugged him last night, they risked doing so since he is still unconscious now."

"What nonsense," said Lady Catherine. "The man is clearly drunk."

"She is meeting with a servant, Mr. Darcy. Surely, you can see how unsuitable Elizabeth Bennet is now?" Caroline's eyes were shining with excitement, and she clearly expected Mr. Darcy to agree and immediately banish Lizzy.

Instead, he was soft-spoken when he said, "I can see what is going on here."

Caroline was practically vibrating with excitement. Lizzy's shoulder stiffened a little, but she realized she wasn't feeling any true anxiety. She was confident Fitzwilliam knew her well enough by now to realize the situation, especially since he was privy to Anne and Carlos's secret. Even if Lizzy were the type to betray their budding romance with someone, it wouldn't have been the man Anne loved, who loved her.

"It is about time," said Lady Catherine as she sneered at Lizzy. "You attempted too far above your station, foolish girl. Had you been content to wait for your shameless deeds, perhaps you might have fooled my nephew, but you shall never fool me. Now his blinders are removed, and you will remove yourself from Pemberley land."

Lizzy straightened her shoulders as she looked at the older woman. "I shall only do that if Fitzwilliam asks me to, and I assure you, he will not."

Lady Catherine drew herself up to her full height, and it was an impressive sight, but Lizzy felt no intimidation. "How could he not send someone like you away?"

"It is perfectly obvious that someone is setting out to ruin Lizzy," said Fitzwilliam in a surprisingly mild tone. He sounded almost unconcerned when he glared at Lady Catherine, and then at Miss Caroline. "I do not know if you are working in conjunction, or if one of you has taken the lead on this scheme, but I consider you both guilty."

Caroline let out a startled screech as Lady Catherine's mouth dropped open in shock. The older woman was the first to recover. "You cannot believe this was a setup, Fitzwilliam? She is here alone with this man in the cottage."

"She was locked in," said Anne then.

Lady Catherine looked dismissively at her daughter. "Miss Caroline already explained she moved the chair there to keep Lizzy from escaping so she could show proof of her betrayal to Mr. Darcy."

"Most convenient," said Anne, her disbelief obvious.

Lady Catherine clearly didn't like being challenged by her daughter, but her attention was focused mainly on Fitzwilliam. "I insist you sever this inappropriate connection immediately. As for the groom, he is fired once he wakes up enough to recover a modicum of sobriety and digest that news."

"I cannot keep you from firing Carlos, but I can offer him a position here at Pemberley, for he is clearly a victim too." Fitzwilliam moved closer to Lizzy, and she admitted it felt good when he put his arm around her waist.

Relief swept through her, and though she hadn't really doubted his faith in her, it was freeing to have it confirmed.

"Lizzy has been the subject of machinations, but she did not meet Carlos like this. She and I were together this morning walking Pemberley, and it was not even fifteen minutes before Miss Caroline came to fetch me that I had parted with her."

Caroline looked vaguely constipated for a moment in her consternation. "I... But..." She trailed off, her mouth closing so rapidly that her teeth clicked together.

"You might condone this sort of immorality, but I assure you, word will circulate of what kind of woman you are courting, Fitzwilliam. If you choose to continue down this path and sully our name, I will have no choice but to disown you."

"I accept your terms, Lady Catherine," said Fitzwilliam formally, though he appeared to be staving off a smile.

"I have never been treated like this," said his aunt, her outrage obvious.

"Perhaps it is time," said Lizzy in her too-sweet tone.

"Anne, come along. We are leaving Pemberley."

"I do not wish to go with you, Mama."

Lady Catherine had already started marching toward the door, and apparently, it took her a moment to realize her daughter was rebelling, because she took a few more steps before freezing and turning to look at Anne with her mouth agape. "I beg your pardon?"

"If it is all right with Fitzwilliam, I will stay here."

"You are welcome to stay as long as you need or like," said Fitzwilliam immediately.

Anne nodded her appreciation before turning to face her mother. "Since you have fired Carlos, you have severed the last impediment between us. You should know that I am in love with him, and we have been meeting secretly for months. I intend to marry him as soon as it can be arranged."

Lizzy felt almost sorry for Lady Catherine as the color drained from her face. For a moment, she looked dreadfully ill, but the old biddy soon rallied, stiffening her shoulders as she glared at her daughter. "If that is true, I disown you as well."

"I fully expected that, Mama. I feel it is timely to remind you I have reached my majority, and according to the terms of Papa's will, my inheritance is now mine to control."

Lady Catherine stumbled then. "What do you mean?"

"I mean, I believe it is time for you to retire to one of our country estates. Carlos and I will likely want to move back to Rosings Park after our marriage."

"You cannot do that." Lady Catherine looked alarmed for the first time. "Rosings Park is my home. Your father built much of it for me."

"Perhaps I would be willing to negotiate your continued residence there. I believe Carlos and I might enjoy traveling for a while anyway, since neither of us have had much opportunity to see all of England. With the continent inaccessible due to the war, I doubt our travels could take more than a year. In that time, you will return to Rosings Park and resign yourself to the change in circumstances. You will find a way to support my marriage to Carlos without attempting to undermine it, gossip against him, or maneuver against me. We will have your full and unwavering public support, or you will find yourself living at the cottage in the Cotswolds."

The color drained once more from Lady Catherine's face. "I despise that property."

There was an impish look in Anne's eyes when she nodded. She sounded calm when she said, "I am aware, Mama. I suggest you remove yourself from Pemberley and begin adjusting your expectations for how your life will go. Furthermore, you will also adjust your expectations for my life, for I will be living as I choose, and not under your dictates."

Lady Catherine managed to rally a little of her dignity, sweeping out of the cottage as though she were a queen, but Lizzy spared only a small glance for her as she rushed over to Anne, taking her hand. "You were magnificent, my dear."

Anne was trembling slightly now, likely in reaction. "I did not know I had that in me. I must admit, I have fantasized a similar scene many times over the years, and they came with increasing frequency after meeting Carlos, but I never expected to actually have the nerve to say the words." After a moment, she glanced at Carlos. "Do you think he will be all right?"

"I believe so, but we could send for an apothecary or the surgeon if you have any doubts," said Fitzwilliam.

Anne hesitated and then sat down on the bed. "I will simply remain here with him to ensure he is all right. If he does not awaken soon, then I might exercise that option."

Lizzy turned away from her, abruptly remembering Caroline was still in the room. The other woman was pale and trembling, and she seemed to be trying to draw in on herself as though she could make them forget her presence. Lizzy smiled at her, and she managed to make it a kind one. There was no point in gloating now that she had won.

Fitzwilliam faced Caroline directly. "You will now be leaving Pemberley as well, Miss Bingley."

She trembled anew, her mouth opening and closing for a moment. "I was trying to save you from making a terrible mistake, Fitzwilliam."

"I fully understand your motives, Miss Bingley, and I tried to be kind while making it clear I would never be interested in taking you for my wife. That you have descended to such a low scheme only proves to me I was right in my assessment. You would never suit me."

"How did you make this work?" asked Lizzy, full of curiosity, and perhaps even a touch of admiration that Caroline had come up with the twisted plot. She admired the other woman's intelligence, though she found nothing likable about her ethics.

"I saw you and Miss Anne acting furtively shortly after her arrival. You both seemed well pleased when you found this cottage, and so I returned to follow you the next day when the two of you were walking. I saw her meeting with the groom," Her voice dripped with disdain as she said the word, "And I considered revealing all then, but I decided it might prove useful for another purpose. When the man entering your room did nothing to dissuade Mr. Darcy, and in fact, he even lied to support your preposterous claims, I knew I had to do something more drastic."

"It was no lie, and it was no preposterous claim. Have you ever known Fitzwilliam to be dishonest, Miss Bingley?" Lizzy kept her tone kind, but she wanted Caroline to realize the full extent of her folly. "There was nothing untoward about the man in my room, because it was me as I claimed. You have disgraced yourself with this plot and lost the friendship of Fitzwilliam Darcy for no reason, for there is nothing you could have done to pull us asunder." She took Fitzwilliam's hand as she said the words, and he squeezed lightly.

"Lizzy has the right of it," said Fitzwilliam, his tone almost gentle. "Your brother will always remain my dearest friend, but you have lost my trust, Miss Bingley. When we meet in future, please remember that, and also bear in mind what your actions have cost you. It is not too late to change if you desire to do so."

Caroline looked gutted as she dabbed at her face with her gloved finger, wiping away tears. She didn't manage Lady Catherine's feigned dignity as she turned and departed, but she didn't protest or try to offer further excuses. Nor did she try to sway Fitzwilliam to change his mind. She must have accepted the futility of the attempt.

After Caroline had departed, Lizzy and Fitzwilliam left the cottage a few minutes later, while Anne remained behind to watch over Carlos until he was fully conscious.

"Thank you," said Lizzy as they walked, her arm entwined with his.

He paused, turning to face her. "For what?"

"For believing and defending me. We had been together this morning, but am I correct in assuming that even if we had not, you would have recognized what Caroline was doing and Lady Catherine was supporting?"

That he nodded immediately was gratifying. "Without question. I know you, Lizzy, and I love and trust you."

Lizzy blinked back unexpected tears as she lifted her head to find his mouth, kissing him passionately. They might have continued on in that vein if they hadn't heard someone running toward them. Lizzy quickly stepped back, though she doubted the footman approaching had been spared seeing her in Mr. Darcy's arms.

The young man stopped, clearly winded, and he took a second to regain his breath. "I am sorry to disturb you, Mr. Darcy, but you wanted me to report to you as soon as I returned from speaking with Madam Childe." The boy blushed, likely having been surprised to be sent on such a task.

Fitzwilliam nodded. "Did she have a message for me, Reams?"

"Yes. She would like you to meet Miss Flora at the tearoom at one o'clock. She assures you she will guarantee Miss Flora's presence."

"Thank you, Reams. You may return to your usual duties."

After the footman had left them, Lizzy and Fitzwilliam resumed walking. "I would like to have a long discussion with you, but I do not want to have it disrupted at a crucial point. I suggest we table any talk until after we have met with Miss Flora. Do you find that agreeable, Lizzy?"

"I think that is a wise plan, Fitzwilliam. I do admire your mind."

He seemed like he was sulking, but there was a twinkle in his eye when he asked, "Is that all you admire about me?"

Lizzy tipped her head slightly, as though considering. "I confess, I do admire your vast fortune, and your ability to wield it so effectively to get what is required."

If he believed a word of it, his expression didn't show it. He merely grinned at her and said, "Minx."

"I hear you are passably good at chess as well, though I have not had an opportunity to prove that for myself yet. Perhaps we can enjoy a game soon? I am quite a formidable opponent, I assure you."

His hand wrapped around hers, and he blatantly grinned. "I have no doubt of that. I estimate there is little you could not accomplish if you are determined to do so."

Lizzy's face flushed at the unexpected sincerity in his tone. It was a little out of place for the lighthearted mood she'd been trying to strike, but she couldn't deny the warmth infusing her, and she cuddled a little closer for a moment, laying her head on his shoulder. "I do like how much you like me as well, Mr. Darcy. That is certainly another point in your favor."

He chuckled. "For as much as I like you, Lizzy, I suggest you might add two points to ensure proper credit."

Chapter Eleven

Lizzy had been in a good mood since this morning, particularly after they had arrived at Pemberley in time to see his aunt and then Miss Caroline depart within moments of each other. Darcy winced now as he recalled the tense and uncomfortable conversation he'd had with Charles, outlining the situation. He'd been afraid it might sever the ties between them, but Charles had sensibly laid the blame at Caroline's feet, supporting Darcy's decision that he could not be in the same social circles as her, at least until he had assurance she was no longer plotting against the woman he intended to marry.

Just thinking about it caused him to look at her now, and he wanted to reach across the table and take her hand, but that would be scandalous in public, even if they were betrothed or married. He contented himself with sending her a warm smile, realizing she was nervous. Her fingers were continuously fiddling with the silver box on the table in front of her, and she was casting an anxious glance almost constantly at the door to the tearoom.

She seemed anxious that Miss Flora wouldn't show up, but Darcy was more confident. He had paid well enough to ensure Madam Childe had good reason to produce Flora. He was unsurprised when a thin, sallow woman entered just a few minutes past one, her posture one of defeat as she came closer to them. He knew it must be Miss Flora by Lizzy's exhale of relief, and the way her shoulders loosened slightly as tension left her.

When the woman sat down, Lizzy stiffened again, but it seemed to be with a new kind of tension, though her voice was neutral when she said, "Thank you for joining us, Miss Flora."

The woman sniffed. "I would not be here if Madam Childe had not forced me. I have nothing to share about Mr. Terrence that will assist you."

Lizzy's tone was gentle. "I suspect there is nothing you want to share. However, I have something I must share with you."

Flora frowned as Lizzy opened the silver box. She looked at the ring doubtfully. "Are you trying to bribe me, miss?"

Darcy started to speak, but realizing Lizzy seemed to have it in hand, he leaned back and let her control the narrative. From the way she acted, he suspected Lizzy had a theory, though she hadn't shared it with him yet. He was irritated by that, and he would take her to task for it later, but for now, he was content to allow her to go with her instincts, since they were usually accurate when it came to solving mysteries.

"We found this among Mr. Terrence's things. As I told Mr. Darcy, I suspect it was an engagement ring."

Flora's hand trembled as she reached for the box, bringing it closer to examine the contents. Tears started to leak from her eyes, though she seemed unaware. "He promised he was going to marry me, but he would not say when."

"You must have quarreled about it?" asked Lizzy in a gentle tone.

"I was desperate, you see? Madam Childe has told me I am getting too old, and if not for Mr. Terrence's patronage, I would have been discharged last year. He claimed to love me, but he kept insisting we wait a while longer, until he had enough money saved to leave service."

"That can take quite a while," said Fitzwilliam in a sympathetic tone, while wondering why Mr. Terrence hadn't come to him for assistance. He knew the obvious answer was because servants were discouraged from having personal lives, but he'd like to think his staff would give him the opportunity to help. Apparently not in Mr. Terrence's case.

"He wanted to open a horse-boarding facility, but there were always promises of soon, soon...and I could not take it anymore. When I told him Madam Childe was turning me out, he promised to speak with her and negotiate a few more months, so I would have a position and could help put toward our savings. I was certain he was lying then, intent only on using me, and based on his promises, I had made no further plans of my own. I believed he would take care of me, and I was so angry. I thought he had lied to me, you see?" Her face was covered with tears now, and her cheeks were blotchy.

Lizzy patted her hand. "I am certain I can understand at least some of your rage. Was it your knife or Mr. Terrence's?"

"It was mine," said the other woman with a small hiccup. "In my line of work, a woman must learn how to protect herself, so I carry it everywhere. I did..." She trailed off, looking lost. "It was out of my garter and in my hand before I even realized it. I do not know how I did such a thing, for it was like something else had possessed me. I was in such a rage, you see?"

Darcy winced, having sympathy for her, though the lion's share was for Mr. Terrence.

"I did not realize he truly planned to marry me." She brushed her face then, using the napkin that had never made it to her lap. "I thought it was just empty promises." She took the ring from the box and put it on her finger, silently crying for a moment. "It is near a perfect fit."

"I am sorry for the situation, Miss Flora. You understand we must turn you over to Constable Smith and the Runner from London?" Lizzy sounded gentle as she shared the news.

Miss Flora was apparently in no state to object. She just nodded, and when Darcy stood up, taking her arm to prompt her to stand as well, she was compliant. He maintained a grip on her bicep as they walked from the tearoom to Constable Smith's office, in case she decided to try to run, but the fight seemed to have gone out of the woman. It was a complete tragedy and a waste of two lives that her rage and Mr. Terrence's clumsy handling of the situation had pushed it to the point where she had killed him.

Constable Smith and Mr. Kenton were speaking in quiet tones when they entered the office a few minutes later. They both seemed surprised to see them, and after Lizzy had briefly explained the situation, Constable Smith took Miss Flora by the arm and led her to the back, where the cell waited. Darcy realized she would have to share with Wickham, and he felt sorrier for her than ever. Her own actions had driven her to this point, but he was still capable of some understanding.

He bore no such understanding for Wickham, and he was almost disappointed to learn the man hadn't been the one to kill Mr. Terrence. He was sorry Mr. Terrence had lost his life, but it had seemed like it would finally ensure the end of Wickham. When Constable Smith returned, he asked, "What will happen to both of them?"

Lizzy moved closer, putting her arm through his, and she seemed just as vested in the answer.

"They shall be presented to the magistrate, of course." Constable Smith seemed to think that was the end of the matter.

Lizzy frowned. "Assuming they are convicted, what will happen to Miss Flora?"

"It is hard to say," said Mr. Kenton.

"Will she hang?" asked Lizzy, her hand clutching Fitzwilliam's arm firmly enough that he felt the pressure with a little wince.

"It is possible, though perhaps she will have a sympathetic magistrate, and she will only receive life in prison instead."

"Hanging might be kinder," said Constable Smith, apparently unaware of how off-putting his brusque tone was.

Lizzy glared at him, saying, "How could life in prison be worse than death?"

The constable shrugged. "If you have not been to Newgate, I shall not enlighten you, Miss Bennet."

Darcy cleared his throat, addressing the question to Mr. Kenton. "What will happen to Wickham?"

"We have him for certain on the thefts, and if Miss Darcy is willing to lay a complaint about the kidnapping, I feel confident we can ensure he is locked in Newgate as well, or perhaps deported to Australia. He is unlikely to hang for his crimes."

Darcy felt a strange sense of relief and disappointment. He realized perhaps he cared more about Wickham than he had considered, for he was unable to completely dismiss that they had grown up together and had once been like brothers. He was glad Wickham wouldn't hang, though perhaps he deserved to, but having him in Australia sounded ideal. "I shall campaign for his deportation."

"I have no doubt you can influence the magistrate toward that direction, Mr. Darcy," said Mr. Kenton

"The lady told me she saw Wickham strewing about the hay and setting the fire as she was leaving the stables after stabbing Mr. Terrence," said Constable Smith. "She volunteered the information when I placed her in the cell with him. You have him on that as well."

Fitzwilliam allowed relief to sweep through him, certain Wickham would pay for his crimes and no longer bother the Darcy family.

Constable Smith moved to his desk, clearly retrieving something, and Mr. Kenton looked at Lizzy then. "I was hoping to have a chance to tell you Mr. Nobles has been remanded to Bedlam. He was declared irredeemably insane and shall likely die there."

Lizzy sagged in relief against Fitzwilliam. He ensured he held her in a bracing fashion.

When it was clear their part in the situation was over, at least for now, Fitzwilliam held onto Lizzy's arm and escorted her from the constable's office. When they stepped out, he drew in a deep breath, appreciating the freedom he had. He had done nothing to risk it as

Wickham and Miss Flora had, but he still appreciated it, nonetheless. Leading Lizzy to the carriage, they were soon on their way back to Pemberley.

Chapter Twelve

After dismissing Mr. Nobles from her mind, realizing she didn't want to waste even a second thinking about him, Lizzy couldn't wait to return to Pemberley for their conversation. Boldly, she moved across the carriage to sit beside Fitzwilliam. "I have changed my mind."

He frowned. "About what, Lizzy?"

"When I once decided I could never imagine marrying you, I realize now that was a foolhardy statement. Circumstances have changed, and I have seen enough of you that I am positive I have not always had a completely favorable or correct impression of you."

He seemed startled by her words. "If you refer to what I think you are referring to, please allow me to state that nothing has changed on my side. If you do not wish me to bring it up again, I will not, but I must fervently and ardently declare my love for you."

Lizzy had heard him say it before, but there was something different and special about it this time. It wasn't surrounded by his insulting words and condemnation of her family. She had no doubt of his sincerity, and she felt like she knew Fitzwilliam and his heart well enough to admit the leanings of her own. "I love you as well, Fitzwilliam. If you wish to reiterate the question you posed in Hunsford, I can assure you it will have a different answer this time."

He turned on the bench to face her, taking her hands in his. "Will you do me the honor of being my wife, Elizabeth Bennet?"

"I will." It was a succinct statement, and Lizzy had planned to say more, but Fitzwilliam had other ideas. He lifted her onto his lap and kissed her soundly, until she could barely remember her own name. She clung to him as the miles between Lambton and Pemberley stretched, bringing them home.

As they rode down the drive of Pemberley, Fitzwilliam apparently managed some modicum of control, and Lizzy appreciated it, because she was incapable of doing so. When he pulled away, she was still clinging to him. They weren't actively kissing, but she sat on his lap when the carriage door opened a moment later, revealing her delighted mother.

"Lizzy, you clever girl. You have ensnared Mr. Darcy."

Lizzy cringed, hating the way her mother phased that, as though it had been some stratagem on her part.

Fitzwilliam surprised her by laughing, sounding indulgent. "She most assuredly did, Mrs. Bennet, but I would like to think I have ensnared her too. I assure you, I will speak with Mr. Bennet at the soonest opportunity."

Fanny was beaming. "Such fabulous news. I will write to the man immediately and insist Thomas join us here." Before she could run off to do so, she paused and took Lizzy's hand. "Congratulations, my dear. We shall have your father here within days, and you shall be a properly betrothed woman." Releasing her daughter's hand, she bustled into Pemberley, crowing with delight about two of her daughters making sound matches.

"I guess she forgot Mary is betrothed too," said Lizzy with a grin as Jane stepped forward. Her sister hugged her as soon as she was out of the carriage, and Lizzy embraced her just as enthusiastically. Fitzwilliam stepped down behind her, his arm around her waist.

"We should get married together," said Jane.

"No," said Fitzwilliam.

Lizzy turned to glare at him. "Why ever not?"

"Your sister and Bingley are planning a Christmas wedding. I cannot possibly wait that long to marry you. If I have my way, we would get a special license and wed in three days, but since we have to wait for Mr. Bennet to arrive so I can formally ask him his permission, I am willing to wait two weeks. Not a moment longer."

Jane seemed to consider that for a moment, and then she nodded. "Very well. I am content to move up the wedding if Mr. Bingley is." As she said that, she threaded her arm through Charles's. "What do you think, darling? It would make me happy to marry at the same time as Lizzy."

Bingley nodded enthusiastically. "It would make me happy not to have to wait all those extra months either, my love. I am content to marry in two weeks if we can make it happen."

"I doubt there is little Mr. Darcy cannot make happen when he sets his mind to it," said Lizzy as she took Fitzwilliam's hand in hers.

"It is reassuring to have your confidence in me at an all-time high," said Fitzwilliam. He seemed on the verge of laughing. "I confess, I still expect you to needle me in some fashion, or find a way to diminish me. That is the nature of our relationship."

She shook her head. "At times, it has been the nature of our relationship, but you are my ally, not my adversary. I am determined we shall have a happy life full of harmonious marital accord. I do not think less of you for having an exceedingly vulnerable spot, and you have been a very good assistant for solving the mysteries that have crossed our path."

He laughed even as he rolled his eyes. "There it is. Just as I expected."

Lizzy beamed. "I would never want to live completely up to your expectations, Fitzwilliam, for life would be dreadfully dull."

He smiled down at her, appearing benevolent. "I have a feeling life will be anything except dull with you, my dear."

Epilogue

Darcy sat beside his bride two weeks later, while her sister was on Lizzy's other side, and Charles sat beside Jane. They shared the head of the table for the wedding breakfast, and the room was full of a mix of their friends and family. Fanny Bennet was seated at the other end of the table, but even from here, he could hear her telling Richard all about the wainscoting in the room, droning on with intricate detail.

He smiled indulgently, surprised to discover Fanny had a way of growing on him. She was overbearing and lacked many of the social graces, but he did not deny she loved her daughters fiercely, even if she didn't seem to quite understand Lizzy all the time. There was a new weightlessness about her that suggested she had been dreadfully strained by concern for her future and her daughters' future that was now to be alleviated by Lizzy and Jane making such smart matches.

His gaze turned to Thomas Bennet, who looked morose as he ate his eggs. The poor man had had a dreadful time parting with Lizzy, but Fitzwilliam had been insistent. Even when Mr. Bennet jokingly offered twice the dowry and both Kitty and Lydia instead of Elizabeth, he had to remain steadfast in his decision to marry Lizzy. His persistence and Lizzy's clear determination, coupled with her obvious love for him, had persuaded Mr. Bennet to accept Darcy's suit, and he had given his reluctant blessing.

Fitzwilliam didn't take it personally, realizing Thomas was likely still adjusting to the shock of not having Lizzy close to him when he had expressed a clear preference for her as his favorite daughter. He would ensure they saw each other frequently, and indeed, it would be good exposure for him too, because he was certain Fanny had already laid claim to the bedchamber she was using as her permanent lodgings once Mr. Bennet died, and she came to live with them.

An idea that would have once filled him with dread was only now a minor prickle of unease, and it was quickly dismissed. Mrs. Bennet was a small price to pay to have Lizzy in his life.

She looked at him now, squeezing his hand. "You seem lost in thought, Fitzwilliam."

He bent his head, keeping his voice deliberately low when he whispered, "I was simply thinking about what happens after our guests leave."

Her eyes gleamed with interest, indicating she was equally enthused about the idea. "I do not suppose it would be polite if we dismissed ourselves early." She sounded regretful.

Fitzwilliam teetered on the edge of encouraging the idea before reluctantly forcing himself to sigh and say, "Frightfully rude. We must endure, but soon, the afternoon will be ours."

She leaned closer, placing her head on his shoulder. "The first afternoon of many for the rest of our lives."

"I quite like the sound of that, Elizabeth Darcy." He liked the sound of that too as he bent his head and kissed her, uncaring if anyone protested the lack of propriety in him passionately kissing his new wife while still at the breakfast table.

This series needs to be read in order, just like Jane Austen's masterpiece.
The series in order:
Rapacity & Rancor[1]
Abduction & Acrimony[2]

1. https://books2read.com/u/4ApM1d

2. https://books2read.com/u/mBwB1k

<u>Extortion & Enmity</u>[3]
<u>Murder & Misjudgment</u>[4]
<u>Perfidy & Promises</u>[5]

PLEASE SIGN UP FOR Abbey's newsletter[6] to receive information about new releases. If you have any difficulties, email Abbey to request a manual add.

---

3. https://books2read.com/u/bxQGPe

4. https://books2read.com/u/bzZyAn

5. https://books2read.com/u/mddaAE

6. https://www.subscribepage.com/JAFF

About The Author

Abbey is a diehard Jane Austen fan and has loved Fitzwilliam since the first time she "met" him at age thirteen upon borrowing the book from the school library. He is the ideal man, though Abbey's husband is a close second. Abbey enjoys writing various steamy and sweet Jane Austen variations, but "Pride & Prejudice" (and Mr. Darcy) will always be her favorite.

Did you love *Perfidy & Promises: A Pride & Prejudice Variation Mystery Romance*? Then you should read *Honeymoon & Hemlock*[1] by Abbey North!

[2]

Lizzy and Darcy are on their honeymoon in Bath when her mother and Kitty show up to surprise them. They have hardly recovered from that shock before they find a dead body in the women's changing room. The waters at Bath might heal, but they can't solve the mystery of who killed Lady Longe, or why they desired the cantankerous old woman's death. Lizzy and Fitzwilliam are the only ones interested enough to investigate the murder by hemlock and find answers. They have a knack for the endeavor, but Lizzy worries Fitzwilliam will lose patience with her undertaking, since it happens to be their honeymoon. *This is a spinoff from Abbey's popular "Crime & Courtship" series, which*

---

1. https://books2read.com/u/mBz7Ay

2. https://books2read.com/u/mBz7Ay

introduced mysteries to their romance. They are now married, but the mysteries continue, as does the evolution of their relationship.While Abbey sometimes writes sensual JAFF, this is strictly SWEET.

Also by Abbey North

A Month To Love
Reproach (Part One)
Resentment (Part Two)
Rapport (Part Three)
A Month To Love Compilation

Crime & Courtship
Rapacity & Rancor: A Pride & Prejudice Variation
Abduction & Acrimony : A Pride & Prejudice Variation Mystery Romance
Extortion & Enmity: A Pride & Prejudice Variation Mystery Romance
Murder & Misjudgment: A Pride & Prejudice Variation Mystery Romance
Perfidy & Promises: A Pride & Prejudice Variation Mystery Romance
Crime & Courtship: A Sweet Pride & Prejudice Mystery Romance Compilation

Darcy's Courtesan
Adversity (Darcy's Courtesan, Part One)

Avidity (Darcy's Courtesan, Part Two)
Amity (Darcy's Courtesan, Part Three)
Darcy's Courtesan: A Sensual "Pride & Prejudice" Variation

Marriage & Mysteries
Honeymoon & Hemlock

Mr. Darcy's Secret Stories
Mistaken Masquerade: A Pride & Prejudice Variation
Mischief & Matchmaking: A "Pride & Prejudice" Variation

Standalone
Christmas At Pemberley: A Pride & Prejudice Variation
A Scandalous Proposition: A Pride & Prejudice Variation
Shadow of Darcy: A Sensual Pride & Prejudice Paranormal Variation
Darcy's Obsession
Blackmailing Lizzy: A "Pride & Prejudice" Variation
Darcy's Wicked Game
Danger With Darcy: A Sensual "Pride & Prejudice" Variation
Passion & Prostrations: A Sensual "Pride & Prejudice" Variation
Darcy's Debt: A Sensual Pride & Prejudice Variation
Obstinacy & Obligation: A Sweet Pride & Prejudice Variation
Darcy's Alibi: A Sweet "Pride & Prejudice" Variation
Marooned With Darcy: A Sensual "Pride & Prejudice" Variation
Compromising Mr. Darcy: A Steamy "Pride & Prejudice" Variation
Marrying Mr. Darcy: A Sensual "Pride & Prejudice" Variation
Darcys' First Christmastide